To
mered...

Follow Me

LESLIE HACHTEL

This is a work of fiction. Names, characters, places and incidents are products of the author's imagination or are used fictitiously and are not to be construed as real. Any resemblance to actual events, locales, organizations, or persons, living or dead, is entirely coincidental.

Follow Me
Copyright © 2024 Leslie Hachtel
Cover Art by Jena Brignola
Interior Design by Judi Fennell at www.formatting4U.com

lesliehachtel.com

Also Available from Leslie Hachtel

Romantic Suspense
Texas Summer
Payback
Once Upon a Tablecloth
Memories Never Die

Notorious Series
Murder Most Notorious

The Dance Series
The Dream Dancer
Emma's Dance
The Jester's Dance
A Dance in Time

The Morocco Series
Bound to Morocco
Tied to Morocco
Freed from Morocco

Historical
The Defiant Bride
Adriana
Hannah's War

Crossover Contemporary/Historical
Stay With Me

Time Travel
Come Back to Me

Acknowledgments

As always, to Jena Brignola for the perfect cover

To Jenn Bray-Weber for always making the book so much better with your brilliant editing

To Bob for his eagle eyes in proofreading

To Judi Fennell who is so amazing at doing everything I can't to get this book published

And, of course, to my readers -

Who graciously accompany me on my journeys.

"When you have eliminated all which is impossible then whatever remains, however improbable, must be the truth."

-Arthur Conan Doyle

Table of Contents

Chapter One

Harper Forbes punched in the entry code on the quaint cottage's front door. Unaccustomed to the damp cold, she was anxious to get inside. Turning back to see the view and the shimmering lochs, she finally appreciated why her best friend Skye wanted to come here. And the castle! Eilean Donen above the dark waters was breathtaking.

It had been a long trip but worry over her friend's disappearance fueled Harper through the journey. Now she was in a foreign country, alone, knowing no one. She refused to let that intimidate her. There were so many questions and Harper needed answers.

The risk was that everything Harper had ever believed about reality might be wrong and she was still debating the merits of actually being here in the first place. Time travel? Seriously? It was a ridiculous concept, but then what had happened to her friend? They were so close, more like sisters, so Harper knew Skye wouldn't just vanish.

It had been weeks since she had received the packages from Skye containing her passport, driver's license, clothes, cash, and even her phone. Skye also sent a cryptic message about the cloak working, and a goodbye. None of it made any sense unless she subscribed to a ludicrous notion about travelling through time. It was more logical that something had happened to her, but then why would she mail those boxes. In fact, some had actually been mailed by the landlord here. After hearing no more for weeks, Harper was too pragmatic to let it go without an explanation.

When she had called the owner of the cottage, the woman Harper spoke to agreed it was strange Skye had her mail the two packages after she left. Harper was told Skye had left very specific instructions. The woman seemed nervous, as if Harper was looking to blame her for something done wrong, but Harper reassured the woman she just wanted some answers as to what had happened to her friend.

Initial concern had built to an urgency and hence her trip here to Dornie and the castle. Now that she had made the trip here, she had no intention of leaving without a viable reason for Skye's disappearance. But the idea of time travel was not in Harper's lexicon. The unknown twirled around in her mind like the wheel in a hamster's cage.

In addition to the worry, Harper missed Skye and found it hard to shake the sadness after she left Memphis. Learning many years ago that action tended to lift the grey smoke of depression, Harper had decided to get on a plane. Her logical side reminded her it might be useless. There were some things she simply couldn't control or discover. Then again, what could a small getaway hurt even if she couldn't find Skye?

Harper had received those packages and it convinced her that Skye had either completely lost herself in fantasy or—and was this even conceivable—had actually traveled back in time. But if Skye had arranged to have her things sent to Harper, where was she now? And how was she managing without identification or money? In 1562? Again—seriously?

Harper set down her luggage and took a moment to appreciate the bungalow. Spacious and cozy at the same time, the accommodations here were welcoming. Plaid shades on the windows were raised to frame the magnificent view of the rolling hills and she was certain that come spring, the fields would boast vivid emerald-green. Of course, she'd be home by then. Unbidden, a chill ran up her spine, but Harper shook it off.

Eilean Donan Castle gleamed in the distance, the ancient walls painted with the golds of the late morning sunshine and reflected in the water surrounding it. It was like looking at a dream within a dream. Yes, that summed it up. A few sparse trees sheltered the stones, which made the edifice even more imposing and unassailable. It was as if it declared "if you are foe, you will not reach us". Exciting and foreboding and promising.

This all started when Skye had found a portrait of a Scotsman painted in the 1500s and she had apparently fallen in love with the man, or at least his image. A little research and it was clear the background of the picture was here, with a backdrop of the castle. Declaring the man her soul mate and determined to find him, Skye had bought a time travel cloak on Ebay, of all places. She could hear Skye now: "their purchases come with a guarantee". Ridiculous! But Skye was not to be talked out of it and had come here, to Eilean Donan castle. And soon after, after sending Harper packages with her belongings and identification, she vanished. That was nearly two months ago. Now it was approaching the winter holidays and that was definitely not Harper's favorite time of the year. If she was being honest, she was looking for an excuse to think about something—anything—else other than "deck the halls". She and Skye had always made sure to spend this time of year together, even when Harper was briefly married, because neither of them had family to speak of, or any warm memories to look back on. So, Skye wouldn't just disappear, especially at Christmastime.

Harper was beyond worried about her friend, the fear and the loneliness, a sharp stick pressing against her heart.

Even with her crazy imagination, Skye was the best friend Harper had ever had. Her fantasies and fairy tales were always stretching the bounds of reality, while Harper was earthbound and practical. Skye's idea of catapulting through time was absurd. But when you eliminated the impossible… was it truly impossible?

Harper picked up her bag and carried it into the bedroom. She'd unpack later. She wanted to wash her face after the long journey.

Harper took a long look in the bathroom mirror above the sink. "Who are you?" she asked the reflection. "Chasing after Skye because she said she could time travel? You know better than that!" Harper sighed. "But where is she?" There was no quelling the constant worry.

A woman's cry carried from the bedroom. Harper immediately startled at the sound of panic in the woman's howl. Rushing out into the next room, she was stunned to see a young woman she didn't recognize dressed in medieval clothes and wrapped in a filthy old cloak. The woman's dark hair floated around her in a mass of tangles and the expression on her face was a combination of confusion and distress. Gauging her to be in her early twenties, the woman nevertheless had the look of one who had seen much of life. Her gown was impressively authentic, and her stance defiant, her hands on her hips, her eyes narrowed.

4

How did this woman get in here? Who was she? Or maybe—maybe—it was all meant to make visitors feel as if they had gone back in time. Part of the atmosphere? Still… it was odd.

Harper might have been annoyed by the intrusion, until her gaze was drawn again to the cloak the woman wore. Harper recognized that cloak. Skye had shown it to her before she left for Scotland. There was no mistaking it had to be the same one. Now more questions buzzed through Harper's mind: how was it this other woman was wearing it? Who was she? Did she mug Skye and steal it? But who would bother robbing anyone for an old rag of a garment? Or was it that jet lag caused hallucinations?

Harper was pretty sure the woman was real and not a figment of her imagination, but how did she just appear here? Harper was certain she locked the front door when she arrived. And did she have any information about what had happened to Skye? Before she could ask anything, the other woman momentarily flashed her gaze at Harper before angling her head and scanning the room.

"Where?" the woman demanded, irritation twisting her features. "What happened?" Her gaze direct and her lips puckered, she glared at Harper as if Harper was responsible. "Did ye bewitch me?" The rancor in her tone was unmistakable.

"What I'm thinking—not possible," Harper said aloud more to herself than to her intruder. "There has to be a logical explanation."

The stranger took several steps away from Harper, but she was too busy looking everywhere at once to answer.

More curious than intimidated, Harper took a step forward. "Who are you? And how did you get in here?"

"This isnae the castle. How *did* I get here? Indeed.

5

How did ye do it?" Her brows came together, forming a crease between her dark eyes—eyes that reflected a lack of empathy. Her tone softened. "Ye must be verra rich to live in this place."

"I don't live here," Harper responded instinctively. "I'm looking for my friend Skye."

"Skye?" The woman fairly shrieked. "Skye?" she repeated. "That *howfin galla.*" Even Harper, who spoke little Gaelic, guessed that a *galla* was a bitch by the venom in the other woman's tone.

"So you know her! Where is she?" Finally, some answers!

"No doubt bewitching the laird—who is mine!" Her reptilian smile made goosebumps rise on Harper's skin. "Make no mistake. I will end her." This last was said on a breathy whisper seething with malice. The woman continued to smile without humor, her eyes also reminding Harper of a snake. "If ye are friends of the lady Skye"—she spit the name as if it tasted like lemons—"and if she is yer caraid, ye are no caraid of mine," she said. "So do tell—who are ye?" the woman demanded, her voice again more a screech.

Harper raised her eyebrows and, determining to stand her ground, stared at the other woman. "I might ask the same of you."

"Davina. Of Clan Mackenzie." This was said with a lifted chin and a thick Scottish brogue.

This was too fantastic to be anything but a hallucination, but that didn't make sense, either. Harper decided that maybe she should just play along. "It is possible I have a problem with her as well. Where is she?"

"And who be ye?" the one named Davina of Clan MacKenzie repeated, annoyance clear in her tone.

"I am Harper of—Clan Forbes. I suppose you expect me to welcome you to the twenty-first century." It just seemed the right thing to say, which was silly.

"The what?" Her puzzlement actually appeared genuine.

"I believe that cloak you are wearing is responsible." *But really, was it?* "It belongs to Skye. Where did you get it?"

Davina gaped down at the cloak as if only now realizing she wore it, then quickly dropped the garment to the floor, kicking it away as if it might bite her. She made her way around the room, out into the living area, and to the front door. Glancing back at Harper over her shoulder, she flung the door wide and stepped outside.

Fascinated, Harper followed, wondering how long this charade would continue.

Davina looked across the loch at the castle and frowned as if dumbfounded. "A bridge? Nay. It wasnae there but a moment ago." Turning to Harper, it was clear she wanted an explanation. "Ye are a witch. I will see you burned."

Shrugging, Harper had trouble taking all this seriously. But she was getting tired of the game this woman was playing. "As I said before, welcome to the twenty-first century. Where did you get the cloak?"

Shaking her head, Davina backed away from Harper, seemingly bewildered, when an airplane passed overhead. Her mouth fell open, and she let out a shriek as she stared skyward. Shuddering in sudden panic, Davina turned and took off at a run across the meadow that separated the cottage from the loch and the castle bridge. The two-lane highway loomed just ahead, but Davina failed to notice the oncoming car, so clearly intent on looking at the castle.

7

Instinct kicked in and Harper took off after her. "Stop! Look out!" But it was too late. There was a screech of brakes and a terrible slamming sound as the vehicle struck Davina, flipping her into the air. Gravity pulled her back to crash into the pavement with a sickening crunch.

Harper ran to her as the driver threw himself out of his car and raced over to them. "I didn't see her. She came out of nowhere." His complexion was blanched with fear, his eyes wide with both guilt and terror. "I didn't see her."

"Call 911. Or 999. Or whatever the emergency number is," Harper ordered the man. Her heart was painfully pushing against her ribs and her breath came hard and fast. Not a usual believer in prayer, she nevertheless found herself asking God not to let this woman die. Convinced this woman was an important part of her search for Skye, Harper knew if she succumbed, Harper would never have the answers she so desperately sought.

***

After giving her statement to the police and watching as the ambulance pulled away, sirens blaring, Harper stumbled back to the cottage as if in a daze. The ambulance driver had told her they were taking the woman to Broadford Hospital and hinted that the chances of her survival were not good. He'd said more, but Harper had been too much in a state of shock to remember. She did recall telling the EMT's the woman's name.

The cottage door was still gaping open, and Harper drifted inside. She sank down on the couch and concentrated on getting her focus back. Fervently wishing she could talk to Skye about what had just happened, Harper broke down and sobbed. That poor woman. No matter who she was, she didn't deserve such a fate. And the man who had hit her. Harper cried for him as well. How terrible to be the driver. Taking deep breaths, she finally calmed and tried to be logical. What should she do now?

In her line of vision, crumpled on the floor, the old, tattered cloak mocked her. Rising from her seat, she walked over to it, and held it up, then carefully brought it back to the arm of the sofa and sat beside it, leaving enough distance so she didn't have to touch it.

"Is it true?" she asked the cape, then felt silly talking to a grimy bit of fabric. That old garment couldn't possibly have the power to transport someone through time any more than it could answer her question. But how could she explain the woman Davina appearing in the cottage in clothes that clearly seemed from another age? And with Skye's cloak wrapped around her.

A thought occurred. Maybe there was a Renaissance faire nearby and the woman had simply walked in here by mistake. But didn't the door to the cottage lock automatically? Harper stood and walked back over to the entry and stepped outside. A rush of icy air lifted her hair and Harper shivered, but she refused to view that as any kind of omen. No matter what, she intended to hang on to facts. Data. Logic.

The lock audibly clicked into place when the door closed. Re-entering the code, she stepped back into the living room. Undoubtedly, the woman couldn't have just wandered in here.

And add to that Harper saw her expression when she spotted the airplane. The woman was terrified and completely baffled. Unless she was an Oscar-caliber actress, Davina was truly discombobulated. So much so, she had nearly been killed. And before that, she had been surprised by the bridge, which had not been constructed until the twentieth century. Without being well-versed in Scottish history, how would she know that? Of course, she might if she actually lived in the area. But the thought of the owners putting on a show for visitors by having actors appear in their rooms—no, that wasn't logical at all.

Desperate for some concrete explanation, Harper inhaled and stroked the cloak. "If you could talk, what could you tell me?"

Folding the garment, Harper took it back into the bedroom and laid it on the bed and stared at it. Holes poked through the worn material, and it smelled of age and wear and being stored in an airless space. Harper denied its potential potency and decided the only answers were to be had at the local hospital. That is, if the woman was still alive and able to talk. There had to be a simple explanation, right?

At the carved oak writing desk in the corner, Harper sorted through some brochures until she found one for a taxi service. She needed to go to the hospital and ask the woman—Davina—her name was Davina—some pertinent questions. Harper at least felt as if she owed it to her—and to herself—to check on her.

The driver pulled up a few minutes later. He was young and very Scottish, a sweet young man in his early twenties with bright red hair and blue eyes. Harper slipped into the back seat and gave him instructions to take her to Broadford Hospital. He was a chatty fellow, which was fine by her. Harper let him do the talking. He told her he was driving to pay his way through college and one day hoped to visit America. As they pulled up to the hospital, he looked at her through the rearview mirror. "I'm glad to say ye do nae look ill. Are ye?"

"What?" The question took her by surprise and she laughed."No. Just visiting—a friend."

"Aye. Good. Well then if after ye would wish to sightsee, I can make meself available. Just so ye know."

"Thanks. I don't know what my plans are, but I will keep in mind that I can call on you." A thought struck. "Is there a Renaissance faire going on around here?"

The man chuckled. "Nay. That only happens in the summer at the castle, to entertain the tourists."

"So no one would be walking around in a costume now?"

"Nay. Why do ye ask?"

"Oh, it's just that I met a woman earlier and she was dressed in an outfit from the medieval time."

"That would be odd. There isnae even a play going on. Soon we will celebrate the holidays, but nae yet."

"And would it be part of the—entertainment—to have someone enter the cottage in medieval dress? To offer atmosphere?"

The boy seemed scandalized. "Nay. That would be rude."

Indeed.

He parked in front, then turned in his seat. "Do ye wish me to wait?"

Harper thought about it for a moment, then decided it might be easier than having to call for another ride. "That would be great. I shouldn't be too long."

***

11

Being a hospital administrator back in the States, Harper was familiar with the setting. The hospital was strikingly similar to her own. Her time at work was spent in the running of a business that provided the same services, but it felt strange to have a personal interest. No one she actually knew had ever been admitted to her hospital.

Making her way to reception, she stopped at the information area and stepped up to the older man behind the desk. Sitting up straighter, he smiled at her. "Can I help ye?"

"An ambulance just brought in a woman from Dornie who'd been hit by a car."

"Name?" the receptionist inquired.

"Davina MacKenzie."

"Are ye related to her?"

"No, but I was there when it happened, and I just wanted to see how she was doing."

"If yer not family, I'm afraid we can't give out any information."

It was not a surprise they couldn't tell her anything. Harper knew this, but she had to try. After all, this was not a normal situation. "Can I at least see her? Please," Harper pleaded.

"I can tell ye she hasnae been assigned a room yet, so she's probably still here in emergency. Ye really can't see her there. But if ye want to check back later…"

"I understand." She was turning away when the man's voice stopped her.

"Well, since she was hit by a car, the police might want to ask you some questions. If ye tell me where they can reach ye, I'll have them be in touch if need be." The man sympathetically shrugged his shoulders. "I'm sorry, but it's the best I can do."

The police had already questioned her at the scene, but she thought she might not have been very coherent at the time, so she didn't disagree. Leaving her information, Harper walked back to the car waiting for her and climbed in. She had no choice but to hope for someone to be in touch or come back here later. The frustration chewed at her.

They pulled up to her door and the boy jumped out to open the back passenger side for her.

"I think I need to stay put for a while, but I might need you later today or tomorrow," she said to the driver.

"Aye. Just ask for Cameron and I'll be at yer service."

But can you drive me to the 1500s? And he would say "sure thing, lady". Or not.

Harper had no sooner sat down on the couch when her cell phone rang. The police would like to come by in two hours to ask her some more questions. With time to wait, she decided she might was well grab some lunch in the meantime at that restaurant down the road. She was starving!

Clachan Pub was the picture of what she had imagined a Scottish pub should be: cozy and warm, with dark wood walls and floor, and a bar that dominated the back wall with bottles of all kinds glittering in the sparse light. It smelled of ale, baking bread, frying meat, and comfort.

A cheery hostess led her to a table in the back and when Harper thanked her, the woman smiled as if she had just realized something.

"Another American girl?" It wasn't really a question.

"Oh, did my friend, Skye, come here?" Knowing that Skye stayed at the cottage, it made sense.

"Are ye talking about that other American girl

13

traveling alone? Auburn hair? Pretty little thing? Women usually come in pairs or groups, so I remembered her."

Harper nodded.

"It was some weeks ago or maybe a month or two, but aye, she was only here the one time. Were ye looking for her?"

"As a matter of fact, I was. She seems to have— disappeared." Harper wondered if she should have said that, but it was too late now. She didn't want things to get blown out of proportion if there was a logical explanation for Skye's behavior. "Well, not so dramatic. I am just not sure where she is at the moment."

The hostess nodded sympathetically. "Oh, I am sorry to hear that. Ye must be a good friend to come seeking her."

"Did she happen to mention where she intended to go after visiting here?" Hope springs eternal.

"Nay. She just seemed to be soaking it all in. And that's the kind of visitor we appreciate."

"She was only here the one time you said?"

"Aye. I suppose she was anxious to see more of the country."

"Yes," Harper agreed, disappointed that the woman had only seen Skye once. There was still a chance Davina would wake up and Harper could get answers from the poor woman in the hospital. "Oh and… have you seen anyone walking about in medieval costumes?"

"Nay this time of year. Only in the summer at the castle. Not even a play is going on."

Her words reinforced those of Cameron. Still, it was possible Davina of Clan MacKenzie had decided to play dress-up for fun, wasn't it?

"Well, what can I get ye?" the hostess asked.

14

Harper smiled at the woman's sweet face, her cheeks pink, and her smile broad.

"Something very Scottish."

***

Her hunger appeased, Harper returned to her lodging and had just settled in when someone knocked on the door. Two police officers, a man and a woman, introduced themselves as Constable Addison and Sergeant Dennie. Harper ushered them to the couch and perched on a chair across from them, hoping the news about Davina's condition was good.

"How is she? Davina." Harper asked.

"Is she a friend of yers?" Constable Addison asked.

"No. I don't know her. I was outside, and she walked up to me. She told me her name and we had barely exchanged pleasantries when she took off running." It was a little white lie, but mostly true.

"Did ye say something to send her off like that?" Sergeant Dennie pressed.

"No. I think there was something to do with the airplane flying overhead." Harper knew this sounded bizarre, but if she told them what she really suspected (did she?) they would lock her up in the insane asylum. "I mean, maybe she had some trauma associated with air travel or something."

"I'm sorry. Are ye saying ye think she was afraid of airplanes?" Addison asked, gazing at Harper as if she had just grown another head.

"I don't understand it myself. I had just stepped outside, thinking about where I should eat lunch, and she approached me. As I said before, she introduced herself, looked up at the sky, saw an airplane, and took off running." Harper shrugged for emphasis.

"Odd." This from Dennie.

"Quite," Addison agreed.

"I thought so, too. How is she?" Harper asked again.

Dennie shot a look at Addison. "In a coma. TBI. May never wake up," he said, nodding as if he hoped that was not going to be the case.

"TBI?" Harper asked.

"Traumatic brain injury. Likely hit her head when she hit the ground." Dennie frowned.

"She did. When the car struck her, she was thrown into the air and landed pretty hard." Harper shivered at the memory and her throat burned. Swallowing hard to quell the nausea, she inhaled.

"Ye have no idea what set her off? Other than an airplane, that is." The skepticism oozed from his tone.

"I can tell you it wasn't the driver's fault. She ran directly in front of his car, and he had no chance to stop."

"Do ye know the man? The driver?" Addison asked.

"No. But as I told you, I saw it all play out. The accident, I mean."

"Tell us again what you saw," Addison asked her.

Harper heaved a sigh. "As I told you, we were just talking, she looked up, a plane was flying overhead, and she took off running as if hell had her."

"Hmmm. I suppose it is possible she was rural and was nae used to planes," Dennie said, with a tone that suggested that would be very unusual. "Do ye ken anything else aboot her? Anything that might have accounted for her reaction?"

Harper shook her head. "Did I mention she was also dressed in a costume from the Renaissance?"

16

"The nurses told us that, as well as the officers who were on scene, but it is odd," said Dennie. "People don't dress up for the tourists this time of year. Unless…"

"Drugs," they both said in unison and nodded.

"That would explain it," said Addison. "Or one of those games like 'Dungeons and Dragons' they play."

"I really have told you all I know. I am sorry she is so badly hurt, though."

"Aye," the two responded, again together. Clearly they had been partners a long time.

"Did she have any identification? A phone?" Harper asked. "Did you notify her family?"

"That's what was so odd. Everyone has a phone these days," Dennie answered. "And her clothes. Garters? Who wears those?"

"Ye would notice those," Addison chided and Dennie had the good grace to drop his gaze. "Well, I guess we'll be having no more answers until she wakes up. If she does, that is."

Standing, they headed to the door. "Are you planning to be aboot for a bit?" Dennie asked.

"I'm not sure. I should be here for a few days, though. I came to find a friend of mine who visited here some weeks ago."

Both detectives stopped cold. "Missing is she?" Dennie asked, eyebrows raised.

"Not exactly." Harper hoped she hadn't said that too fast. But the last thing she needed was for the police to start asking questions she couldn't answer. What could she say? That she thought Skye was right here but in the 1500s? Right! "She came here on vacation and I'm just trying to meet up with her." True enough, sort of.

"Can ye manage to stay here for at least another day? In case we have more questions?" Addison asked.

17

"That won't be a problem. Come by anytime. Or call me in case I'm out sightseeing or something."

"Will do," Dennie said.

Harper held the door open for the two officers as they slowly walked out. A chill breeze whooshed in, and the damp cold seemed to penetrate Harper's bones. Leaning back against the door as she closed it, Harper's thoughts swirled.

The woman, Davina, who had appeared so suddenly in her bedroom was in a coma, so there would be no answers forthcoming from her, at least not for a while. But the very fact that she had appeared in clothes from another era and wrapped in the cloak that Skye had sworn would take her back in time—what was Harper to think?

Logic demanded data. What if Harper followed what Skye told her she planned to do before she left Memphis? Harper could buy some clothes that wouldn't look completely out of place in a medieval setting and do some real research about life in sixteenth century Scotland. Then she could wrap herself in the cloak—the cloak?

Harper raced into the bedroom. The forlorn garment lay where she had left it earlier and Harper lifted it, this time with more reverence. Admonishing herself for giving in to the fanciful turning of her thoughts, Harper took a deep breath. "Is it possible?" she asked herself, not for the first time. "Only one way to find out. But not quite yet. I'm not sure I even want to know."

Chapter Two

1562 Scotland – Eilean Donan Castle

Daimh MacRae was comfortably cool, even though the mid-December temperature would have frozen a lesser man who stood outside without a shirt. Most days, like today, were spent on the training field, fine tuning his muscles, and working off his frustrations. If the need should arise, he wanted to be ready to defend the clan. After the Battle of Corrichie, the winds of war among the Scots had calmed, but that didn't mean the warriors should ever let down their guard. It seemed clans were never satisfied with peace.

He was a large man, his size alone intimidating most everyone, especially the lasses. That served him well as a constable of the castle. A few of the wumman viewed him as a challenge, a game to win, but that wasn't what he desired. But then, a woman who would want him, knowing his secret, was a dream he could never attain.

Laird Ian was happily marrit to the beautiful Skye. Conall was ready to wed the once shy and plain and now lovely Freya, who had proved her mettle in saving Ian's lady when Skye had been secretly imprisoned into the dungeon and nearly died.

The villain who had been responsible for

imprisoning the Lady Skye with the intention of letting her die had also brought plague to the clan. Luckily, Lady Skye had brought medicine from France and saved the poor lad who had sickened, and Lady Skye was freed, but the offender had yet to be found and punished. 'Twas as if Davina had disappeared into the winter air. Rumors abounded, but no one had actually seen her since her guilt was uncovered. Perhaps she truly was a witch as many of the women claimed.

But Daimh's thoughts returned to the sad fact he remained alone. And, although he hated to admit it, he was lonely. Especially this time of year.

He had been told he was handsome, with his dark hair and blue eyes, if he could believe the woman who gave birth to him, but his size and constant frown sent people scurrying. Anyone who really knew him, however, also knew he had a heart that melted at the sight of a child or an injured animal. That was a side he showed no one but his closest friends. It would not do for his enemies to get wind of such vulnerability. Or find out what he was so careful to hide. No one in the clan, save the laird and the two who protected his secret, would be accepting of that truth.

Today, for some reason, the knowledge that he had no wife to love him and warm his bed was affecting him. It could be that the clan was busy planning Conall's wedding, the excitement palpable, or that the holidays were fast approaching. Another Hogmanay without any prospects for the new year.

Was it possible he would get lucky, like Ian, and the perfect woman would appear? Maybe the faeries would forgive him, return what they had taken, and allow him happiness. But that would be a rare occurrence indeed.

With that thought, he picked up his claymore and struck at the hay stuffed scarecrow to release his emotions.

After several more hours of training, weary and hungry, he strode back to the castle into the main hall. Before he could make his way to a table, Iona stepped up behind him and wrapped her arms around his waist. She was bonny enough, with her dark red curls and brown eyes, and her bosom was generous, but he had no interest in her as a mate. She and her mother kept his secret safe and he was grateful, but appreciation only went so far. She had made it clear she would be willing to accept him if he thought to wed her, but he could not pretend love for her.

Her late husband had been a childhood friend and Iona had always seemed more like a sister. And taking his dead friend's widow to wife felt wrong. These were certainly not the kinds of emotions a man should have for a woman he wished to wed. He knew she wouldn't dare betray him or do Thomas any harm, but gratitude for that was not enough of a reason to marry.

"Ye have not been by to visit," the woman purred, leaning into him. "Ye are missed."

He unlatched her hands and turned to her.

"Aye, I hae been remiss. I shall bring ye food and blankets tomorrow. How is he?"

"He is well. A worry, but nae a problem. I must see to me work, what with the wedding and all. But you promise to visit on the morrow?"

"Aye."

Watching her walk away, hips swaying, he dearly wished she appealed to him. But he had a fanciful side that yearned for more. He was a born storyteller and those tales of love he recited had made him yearn for more in life than just settling.

21

Chapter Three

Jet lag hit with the force of a hurricane. Not only was the time difference affecting her, but so much had happened on her first day, Harper was exhausted. Taking a quick shower, she fell into bed and was sound asleep before she knew it.

Her dreams took her to Eilean Donan castle hundreds of years in the past. She was standing in a huge hall all alone. Curiosity pushed her forward, noting the portrait on the wall of the man who Skye had called her soul mate. Staring at it, she sensed someone with her and turned, thrilled to see Skye. Harper reached out to her friend who disappeared in a wisp of smoke, leaving Harper to grasp empty air.

"Soon," Skye's voice whispered from the dream shadows. "Just believe."

Daylight streamed into the room and washed across the bed, prying Harper's eyes open. Sitting up quickly, the dream had spooked her, but she noted she was still in the cozy cottage, and it was cold. She had forgotten to adjust the thermostat before bed last night and the temperature in the room had dropped considerably.

Harper found the switch on the bedroom wall and stood below a vent as lovely warm air washed over her. She realized she was starving, having skipped dinner last night. It was already ten, so she dressed quickly and hurried across to the castle bridge, making her way to the Eilean Donan coffee shop.

As advertised in the brochure in the cottage, the coffee was delicious and it was hard to choose among the pastries, but she decided on a scone with clotted cream. It was so good, she opted for another. After breakfast, she wandered over to the tourist center and bought a ticket for a tour of the castle the following morning. Not quite ready to attempt wrapping herself in the cloak, Harper thought it a good idea to check out the castle itself. A little more time before her cloak experiment would allow her to find answers that made sense and she could drop this whole time travel nonsense. Then again, it was a good idea to see where she might be going if it turned out to actually be possible. What was that quote? "When you have eliminated all which is impossible then whatever remains, however improbable, must be the truth".

Her appetite sated and the tour booked, Harper went back into Dornie and strode among the shops. It was obvious the tourists here loved the history that surrounded them. Authentic tartans abounded in kilts, wraps, and even pillows, along with some period costumes. If she intended to travel back in time, she would need proper attire. It wouldn't hurt to get in the spirit, would it?

Finding an outfit that would not stand out in the sixteenth century was not the challenge Harper had expected. Tartans had not been specific to the clans until the eighteenth century, so she needn't worry about choosing the wrong one. Knowing she might need some explanation as to her origins, if this turned out to be more than just a fantasy, she decided to go with something plain. She found a dark gray long woolen skirt and a heavy linen cream-colored shirt, with a long sleeved over-vest that tied across the chest. A leather belt completed the ensemble. The saleswoman assured her this would be the fashion in any medieval time. Harper thought to ask if the woman had been back in time in order to make these assurances, but decided against a comment that would, no doubt, seem snarky.

Adding woolen leggings with garters and a warm velvet, wool-lined cloak would help protect her from the bone-chilling cold. She also bought a large leather purse with a fold over closure that looked like it might have been made by hand. She initially had chosen a leather bag with an inside pocket that zipped closed. Did they even have zippers in the sixteenth century? A quick Google search on her phone said no, so she chose another bag with a small inside pocket instead.

The niggling fear that she was crazy was dismissed with the thought this was going to simply be for fun, like pretending with Skye when they were children. Only Harper hadn't ever really gotten the hang of pretending. She was too practical for that kind of nonsense. And yet, here she was, playing dress-up.

Satisfied she had what she needed for her costume, she stopped again at the Clachan Pub for dinner. The same hostess greeted her like an old friend, which was lovely. The food was very different than she was accustomed to, but it was delicious. Never a fan of beer, she found that the local ale was a very hearty and pleasant drink, and the atmosphere definitely put her in the proper frame of mind.

It was unnerving to try suspending her disbelief, but if there was any other explanation, she couldn't imagine what it would be. Imagine. That was the key word. Could she really stretch her mental muscles so far as to incorporate fantasy? Well, she decided she had to try. It was, as she had thought of it earlier, an experiment. Once it failed, which she was certain it would, she could look for other answers.

Returning to the cottage, she stared at her luggage. What was she going to do with the suitcase, though? Leave it? It wasn't as if she brought anything irreplaceable and if she left a note, maybe the landlord would store it for her. Or there was Cameron. She bet he'd be willing to take her to some sort of storage facility. If she was going to play make believe, she needed to go the whole way. It reminded her of that movie *Somewhere in Time*. To enable the hero to travel back to meet his love, all the pieces had to make sense. And just like any self-respecting trial, she needed to control as many elements as possible. So, storing her belongings would support the idea this was actually going to work.

"Are you listening to yourself?" she asked out loud. "You actually sound as if you believe all this." But the image of Davina appearing out of nowhere and so clearly confused was a vision she couldn't shake. And the woman seemed to know Skye. Hated her, even. Which led Harper to believe Skye had found the man in the portrait, a man Davina wanted for her own.

Harper's thoughts drifted back to the practical. There was her own license, cash, passport, and phone and Skye's as well, which she had brought with her. She could tuck them into the pocket of the small bag she had bought. Then she would just have to be very careful about not letting the bag out of her sight, but that might not be possible. Or maybe she could just store everything in a locker for a few days, except the cloak of course.

But what else to take? Clean underwear? No, women didn't even wear panties back then. Or bras. All her toiletries were in plastic and how could she explain that? She'd have to do away with these modern day necessities. Deciding she should just use the satchel to tuck away the cloak when she arrived where she was going, Harper walked over to the couch and sat back down, trying to fathom all the necessary answers she might need. And a backstory.

Skye had said she needed a believable backstory, since one could not simply appear at a castle out of the blue without raising suspicions. Harper strained to recall Skye's invented history.

Skye had told Harper she was going to say she had been born in Scotland but had moved to France. Skye spoke passable French, enough to get by. And Harper was actually fluent in the language. She had always hoped her parents would allow her to go with them on one of their many jaunts, and being able to speak in other tongues could prove an incentive to them. It had never worked, but now the skill might actually be useful.

Harper could say she was Skye's childhood friend who had been living in France and had been searching for her since she left. True enough. And Harper's excuse for traveling alone? She could say she was escorted to the castle and felt safe enough to dismiss her companions.

If Skye was there, at Eilean Donan, she would back up Harper's story and welcome her. If not? But where else could Skye possibly be? Lost in space? Caught between worlds?

"Stop it! One test at a time!" Harper admonished herself. It was tough enough to swallow the idea of time travel. She had to believe that if Skye had indeed managed somehow, she would have ended up where she intended. Logical.

Pleased she had created enough of an excuse for her presence at the castle, if she really did go through time, Harper needed yet another excuse for her short hair? So what would be Harper's reason as to why she had cut off her hair? She knew the real answer. When Skye left, Harper wanted a change. So she waltzed into a hairdresser and told them to chop it all off. Well, chin length. She really liked it—sort of—since it was so unlike her to make a quick decision about such things. Now she absolutely regretted it. She was faced with how to explain it in a time when women prided themselves on their long, luxurious locks, like Skye's.

A nunnery. That was the answer. She had been sent to a nunnery but left there to find her friend before she took her vows. Of course, they would have asked her to cut her hair.

Clothes obtained, story in place, and decision made, what else was there? What had she forgotten? Well, except her sanity?

***

Spending the next morning at Eilean Donan was an immersion in history. Armed with another of those fabulous scones to nibble, Harper had opted to take the full tour and the guide was incredibly informative. Built as an island, it sits where Loch Duich, Long Loch, and Loch Alsh meet. The tour guide spoke of the violent history of the place and how it was reduced to ruins, then rebuilt again and again, sometimes larger, sometimes smaller. It had been named for a Gaelic priest, Saint Donnán of Eigg who lived around 580 AD and was martyred trying to bring Christianity to the Pictish people of northwestern Scotland. Since the castle had been here since the thirteenth century, just walking around was impressive.

Apparently there were two ghosts that walked the halls. "Carlos" was a Spanish soldier garrisoned at the castle as they supported the resident Jacobite soldiers, and his footsteps can often be heard by the staff. He is joined by "Lady Mary" who seemed to confine herself to the bedrooms. No one is certain who the lady was or how she had died. And there were so many other stories from the past.

There was also the tale of the laird whose wife seemingly appeared out of nowhere. She was the love of his life, and wherever she went, magic happened. Like "Lady Mary", no one seemed to have known her origins, but she gave him two fine sons and a daughter.

Harper gasped at that and several of her fellow tourists turned and raised eyebrows at her. "That last story," Harper piped up. "The laird and his wife. When was that?"

"Oh, somewhere during the sixteenth century I believe. In fact, that is supposed to be the woman, painted by a C. MacKenzie." He pointed to a painting in a slightly recessed alcove.

Harper stepped closer and blinked, then gasped again, this time so loud the others in the group gaped at her. It was clearly the same artist as Skye's painting. Harper's heart pounded so hard she was afraid the people staring at her could hear it.

Skye? Could it be? The woman was a ringer for Harper's friend, only she was dressed in a gown that was straight out of a Renaissance faire. Harper had to press her lips together to keep from laughing at loud. It was unbelievable.

28

"No one is certain what happened to the picture of the laird, her husband," the guide continued. "It was lost many years ago."

Harper knew the answer. It was still in Memphis, Tennessee.

So far, there had been too many coincidences to ignore. There was almost enough data to wrap herself in the cloak and try it out. Still, Harper held to her skepticism. She wanted to try speaking to Davina once more, just to reinforce... what? An impossible, even ridiculous belief?

Harper returned to the cottage and laid out the period clothing she had bought. After staring at it for minutes, hours maybe, she knew the real question was—what did she have to lose by trying the cloak? The humility of failure. But who would know? And one possibility would be finally eliminated and she could move on in her search for her friend.

She realized she was hungry again. She went back to the pub and fortified herself with a huge plate of fish and chips for lunch, foregoing the ale for a glass of whiskey. If she wasn't careful, she would have to have her new clothes altered. But, when in Rome... And the brisk air and bone-cold temperatures burned lots of calories, right?

Once back inside the bungalow, she tried to calm her thoughts, but her blood was pumping fast and the fear threatened to envelop her. She was faced with taking action or opting for inaction. What if it was real? What if she was actually transported back more than four hundred years? What would she do there? Did she wish to convince Skye to return to the present with her? Harper mulled that over for a while and decided she would never want to deny her best friend happiness. Or a soul mate if she had actually met the man in the portrait. And the tour guide had said she married him and gave him three children. So, it appeared she stayed on. Or—there was that nugget of logic again—the woman in the portrait in the castle was just one of Skye's relatives and the resemblance plausible. But that didn't make sense, did it?

If the cloak actually worked, all Harper had to do was reassure herself that Skye was there and safe and happy and then she could return to the present. She reminded herself she would still have the cloak so she could always come back. In theory, anyway.

Fantasy was hard. How did Skye manage to immerse herself in it? Well, Harper was about to find out. One more trip to the hospital to see if any answers were forthcoming and then... ready or not...

***

1562

Skye and Ian were sitting by the fireplace when Daimh strode into the great hall.

"Laird, my lady," he greeted them.

"Is all well?" Ian inquired.

"Aye. 'Tis quiet again tonight. Hoping that does nae bode the calm before the storm."

"The holidays approach," Ian responded. "Mayhap the clans hae decided to honor our Lord and have peace."

The clans were always at odds, ready to avenge a wrong or take over lands occupied by another. Or for reasons long forgotten, but still inspiring conflict. Coming together at Corrichie had so many clans laying down their arms against one another to fight a common enemy. But the peace between them was always uneasy and never lasted.

Skye sat back in the chair and sighed.

"My love?" Ian inquired.

"I was just thinking of my friend. I miss her and I wish she could share in my happiness." Stroking her belly, she sighed again.

Daimh nodded knowingly. "Yer gift to the laird—when will it be delivered?" he asked.

Her mouth opened with surprise. "How did ye know?"

"Anytime one of the women rubs her belly like that, a child is soon to follow." Smiling once more, he clasped his hands together. "No wonder the laird has been so happy lately." He winked at Ian.

Although Daimh's greatest fear, one he never shared to any but Ian, was that if he were to marry, he might father a child just like the one his mother bore and be dealt with yet another curse of the faeries. Ian always tried to reassure him, but Daimh could not quell the worry.

"Aye, the summer shall see yet another MacKenzie," Ian said, swelling with pride.

"I am so happy for ye." And Daimh meant it. His friend's good fortune only deepened his longing for a wife and family of his own. Ah, but wasn't this the time of year when miracles happened, and one ne'er knew what was in store. Mayhap he, too, might find some luck.

This year, just as the last two, Christmastide celebrations had to be kept secret. After 1560, the reformed Church of Scotland abandoned all Catholic beliefs and rituals in favor of a simpler, "purer" form of worship and a stricter way of life. There was no room in

Presbyterian worship for "popish" ceremonies and festivals such as Yule, now commonly known as Christmas and thought to be pagan. Since the Protestant Reformation, the celebration of Catholic Mass was punishable by penalties, including even death.

But all the restrictions imposed could not change a man's heart and Daimh hoped that the sanctions wouldn't lessen the possibilities for wonders. And there was still Hogmanay, which was a yet politically untouched celebration so far as it only welcomed in the new year. Why he suddenly felt so hopeful was a mystery, but one he intended to hang onto as long as possible, or until it came to fruition.

"Where is yer friend?" Ian asked Skye. "Mayhap she could come for a visit. She would be most welcome here."

"I fear the distance is far too great and I cannot hold out any hope of that possibility."

"Tell us about her," Ian encouraged. Daimh leaned in closer, anxious to hear of another lass. Someone new was always exciting, especially when he was well acquainted with the lasses who lived here.

"She's verra comely. Fair hair and blue eyes. And verra smart. And kind." At the description, a wave of pleasure filled Daimh's chest, surprising him. Was her friend's visit a possibility?

"Well, if ye can manage to send her a message and get her to visit, I think I would like to meet her. And I would wager Daimh would as well."

"If only that were possible." Lifting her shoulders in a shrug, Skye shook her head. "So, since this is my first Christmastide here, do tell me what it's like."

Ian scooted his chair closer to his wife. "Before the

32

Reformation, there was dancing and games and feasting, and the wine and ale flowed. But since the ruling that all things of the Roman Church are now a transgression, we must keep the celebrations more subdued. Until Hogmanay, that is. That is still a festival," Ian explained.

"Well, mayhap that is when you shall find your lady love," Skye teased Daimh. "And do nae deny it. I ken you are ready to settle down. Is there anyone who hae caught yer fancy?

"Nay, me lady. Most of the lasses shy from me, but I hae not given up hope. The laird himself was in despair until ye entered his life. I could get as lucky. And if I recall, ye arrived around Michaelmas, the feast to celebrate angels."

"Aye," Ian agreed. "And how appropriate. I celebrate every day."

"I dinnae understand. Why should any lass not chase you? You are strong and honorable and kind. To say naught of how handsome a warrior ye are."

Daimh's eyes widened at the unexpected praise from the wife of the laird. "I am big, and I think many believe I am dangerous."

Skye grinned. "Only to yer enemies." She shook her head. "If you find a lady to your liking, let me know and I shall put in a good word."

Daimh fervently wished that was even possible.

Chapter Four

It was now mid-afternoon and once more. and perhaps for the last time, Harper was on her way to the hospital to check on Davina. If the woman was awake, perhaps she could finally answer Harper's questions and ease some of the turmoil. Then she could put all this time travel nonsense aside and concentrate her efforts on finding out where Skye had really disappeared to.

The car pulled up out front and she instructed Cameron to leave if she had not returned in twenty minutes. She'd contact him again when she needed to return to the cottage.

Walking inside to the reception area, she asked for Davina's room number. The woman at the desk typed something into her computer and looked up. "I'm assuming yer not a relative," the woman said, raising her eyebrows.

"I was the witness to her accident. I was just concerned for her since she apparently has no relatives here. At least the police told me they hadn't located any so far."

The desk nurse appeared skeptical. "There are MacKenzies everywhere here, so I imagine one of her relations is aboot. But I suppose it wouldn't hurt for you to see her. She's upstairs in the ICU. Third floor. Just follow the signs. The nurses there can help you."

Rather than call attention to herself by approaching the nurses' station, she walked down the third-floor hallway looking into the rooms. She passed several before she saw the woman she sought. Surrounded by machines and hooked up to them by a myriad of wires, Harper quickly checked the corridor. No one was paying any attention to her, so she slipped into Davina's room and stood for a moment looking at her. Watching her rhythmic breathing, controlled by mechanical means, made Harper sad. But then, it was modern technology that might save her. Her dark hair highlighted the woman's pallor, and she might have looked like she was merely sleeping if the machines didn't reflect every aspect of her body's responses. Davina didn't appear any different than any other twenty something woman and Harper wondered what she expected to see. A sign that read 'I'm From The 1500s'? If only the woman would open her eyes.

The tube coming from Davina's mouth was evidence that waking up was not going to be soon, so Harper turned to leave when a thought struck.

Easing her way to the closet on the left side of the room, she opened the door and peered in. Davina's clothes were folded in a plastic bag and Harper reached in to pull out the garments. The materials felt strange, and the clothes were put together with rough hand-sewn stitching. Either this gown was made without a sewing machine, or it was made before sewing machines were invented.

Harper tucked the clothes away, closed the closet, and, with one last look, slipped out. She nearly collided with a man who had appeared just outside the room, his back pressed against the wall to the right of the door. His expression was one of someone who was so defeated he might never recover. And then Harper recognized he was the man that had hit Davina. He was a handsome man in his early fifties, tall and broad-shouldered, with dark hair threaded with white. His eyes were a startling blue-gray and shadowed with grief. Her heart ached for him. Slowly, she approached him.

"It wasn't your fault," Harper said gently.

His eyes flickered, then widened with recognition. "Ye were there." He dropped his gaze, but not before she saw his eyes were swollen and red-rimmed from crying.

"I was. And I told the detectives you aren't to blame. You didn't even have time to react, let alone stop. She ran directly in front of your car." Harper reached out and patted his shoulder. "I'm Harper, by the way."

"James. James MacRae." He looked up, his expression perplexed. "But why was she running? And why into the road?"

"I don't know. Something must have frightened her." Hesitant to ask, but knowing she must, Harper continued. "Have you heard any more about her condition?"

"They don't know if she will ever wake up. She banged her head pretty hard… and so much blood." His voice caught on a choked sob.

"You mustn't blame yourself. It wasn't your fault," she repeated, hoping to soothe away his doubt..

"Thank you, but I was the one who did this to her. And she's a MacKenzie. It has always been the sworn duty of a MacRae to protect MacKenzies."

"You know, sometimes accidents do happen and there's nothing you can do to prevent them. They are just that. Accidents. You mustn't blame yourself."

"And who should I blame? The fairy folk? Thank you for your words, but they canna take away my responsibility here."

Harper nodded and turned. There was nothing she could say to comfort this man. That type of chivalry and moral compass was woefully missing in most of today's society. But she would wager that if it existed here, in present day Scotland, it was no doubt even stronger in this country in the past. If she had been the one driving, she would have felt exactly the same. And Davina was still in a coma, she couldn't offer any reassurances to either one of them.

Grateful the car was still waiting outside, Harper hopped in and went back to the cottage. Cameron indeed knew of a place for her to keep her luggage, so he waited while she picked up her belongings and they rode to the storage facility. Harper rented a space for the three-month minimum. Of course, she would be back to claim her things before then, but she knew they would be safe until she returned. She kept some of her cash, knowing she would need to eat a meal and take care of Cameron. Then they drove back to the bungalow where she paid Cameron and gave him a generous tip. She told him she would call for him again in a few days. *Or would she? Not from the 1500s. Ha!*

It was time to consider her options. But there was only one choice. When you have a theory, you either need to prove or disprove it, right? So the time had come. She just wished she had more data, but there was no more to gain. It came down to a leap of faith. Like when she was little and decided to jump off a diving board into the swimming pool for the first time. Sometimes you just have to close your eyes and push forward and hope for the best.

At the pub, she filled up with a good meal. Harper stared into the second glass of rich amber liquid and fervently hoped to find direction in its depths. Taking a sip and enjoying the slow warmth the liquor imparted, she knew the only answers she was going to find were to first believe in the power of the cloak and see if it actually worked. Not that she really had any real expectation that it would. But at least she would have tried and could move on.

Swallowing the last of the drink, she paid her bill and walked outside into the icy air. The shock of wind cleared her head and refocused her thoughts. Her mind vacillated back and forth on the ridiculous versus why the hell not' until the decision was made.

Seeing Davina's clothes had finally convinced her. The evidence was becoming hard to deny. Stoking her determination as she headed back to the cottage, she reminded herself it would work or it wouldn't. But she had to attempt it. And if it failed?—when it failed!—she would figure out a way to actually discover what had happened to Skye.

Her friend had so much faith in the whole cloak/time travel thing. If Skye hadn't been successful, she would have been horribly disappointed. But how disappointed was the question? Enough to simply give up and disappear? Skye had no identification, no passport, no money. She had sent it all to Harper. And in this day and age, one couldn't simply vanish. Harper would have to enlist the police to find Skye and pray her friend hadn't done something stupid or dangerous or reckless. Until then, she was going to exhaust the other possibility first. The one she couldn't tell anyone else about. There was no question she dared not mention the possibility of time travel to the authorities.

Pacing back and forth in the living room, she finally

faced her remaining reluctance and headed to the bedroom. She laid out her purchases and undressed. One by one, she put on the woolen stockings, shirt, skirt, and other accessories. Checking in the mirror, the lack of bra and underwear wasn't obvious. It would take some getting used to, but she had to admit she was more comfortable. The long skirt whispered around her ankles, and she just felt silly. Like the only one to show up at a party in costume, thinking it was supposed to be a masquerade. But—in for a penny, in for a pound.

Swinging the warm velvet cloak over her shoulders and pressing the bag to her chest, she felt ready. Well, as ready as she would ever be. Even knowing she would need someplace to store Skye's cloak—if it worked—she was aware of how empty the satchel was. All her other belongings were in storage, and she had a moment of panic. But she reassured herself that when she woke up in the morning, Cameron could drive her back to the storage unit and she could retrieve all that she had brought with her.

It was go-time. She grasped the tattered piece Skye had bought on Ebay. She never liked dealing with the unknown and the thought shook her to her core. What if fantasy was about to become her reality?

Wrapping herself in the old material, Harper laid down on the bed, keeping the cold terror that seeped into her bones at bay with sheer will. Turning out the lights and holding onto her bag, she chanted "1562, 1562", believing the cloak needed instructions as to their destination, and wondering when she had actually, irrevocably lost her mind.

Chapter Five

Sleep came immediately and again the dreams were strange, but different than before. First there was utter darkness. Then a swirling, dizzying sensation much like being on a rocking boat, followed by a headache, colors, darkness again, cold. And then piercing light, forcing her eyes open.

Blinking, Harper realized it must already be morning and scoffed at her own naivete. Of course it didn't work. The headache from the night before persisted and she blamed the second glass of whiskey. Never a drinker, she shouldn't have indulged, but she had needed it to calm all her skepticism and suspend disbelief. She also must've slept wrong. She didn't recall the bed being so lumpy. And the stench. What was that smell? Decayed earth and animals? And why was wind blowing into the room? Did she leave a window open? Had she really been so drunk?

She slowly sat up in bed and looked for the source of the breeze. She gasped and her heart threatened to burst from between her ribs. What the hell? Did she sleepwalk? Did the cloak or her own imagination cause hallucinations? She was in a filthy room with a mud floor and a door threatening to pull away from its hinges. Hinges not made of metal. Well, this was a hangover for the books.

Instinctively throwing the ancient fabric from her

shoulders, she stood on shaky legs. It was freezing in here, but she was reluctant to wrap herself in the old cloak again, even if it might provide additional warmth. Setting aside her bag, she moved to the entrance and looked over at the castle. The misty air and the cold drizzle obscured the view, so surely it was a trick of the light glistening off the lochs but the bridge was gone. And so were the paved roads leading to it. This was definitely one hell of a hangover.

Despite the cold, sweat ran down her back and between her breasts. *Not possible* was the refrain on repeat through her mind. The icy air was made more evident in the rush of wind that lifted her hair from her face and helped soothe the headache that still persisted. Her thoughts were at war. Reality versus what she was seeing—and smelling. She needed clarity, a touchstone to steady her mind. Leaning against the sagging doorframe, she looked up at the dark gray clouds chasing each other across the sky. Was she hoping they would part and reveal an airplane?

Harper turned at the clip-clop sound of approaching hoofbeats. A very large man atop a very large horse was coming up the rutted dirt road. His head was down, but when he lifted it and caught sight of her, he slid backward off his mount in slow motion. The ground seemed to vibrate with his fall and the metal from his weapons clanked in the quiet morning air.

Not taking the time to think, only to react, Harper ran to the man and knelt beside him, ignoring the damp that seeped into her clothes. She carefully cradled his head in her lap. His eyes were closed, and his sensuous lips were curled in a half-smile as if he had just tasted something sweet. He was incredibly handsome, with a sculpted jaw and long lashes. The muscles in his arms and chest strained against his linen shirt and vest of sorts. His bare thighs and legs peeked from under his kilt were brawny, like those of a warrior, reminding her of Jason Momoa. Long hair teased his collar, and his sun-darkened skin completed the vision. Only he was in the flesh. Was he an actor? Was this man really here? Or was he just another figment of her imagination?

The tingles in her stomach raced up to her chest.

"Are you all right?" she whispered. "Please be all right."

Opening his eyes and looking up at her as if she were an extraterrestrial being, he grinned. "Did I die?" he asked.

His eyes were so startlingly blue, she inhaled several times to keep from falling into them. She'd heard that expression before, probably in some romance novel, but this was the first time she'd ever experienced anything like it. Or maybe the fluttering in her veins was all part of the hallucination. Yes, that had to be it. It was as if she had known him for an eternity and loved him even longer. But that was as ridiculous a notion as—everything else here.

Remembering his question, Harper shook her head and smiled. The man was dressed as though he was attending a Renaissance faire, complete with the hilt of a sword peeking out from his back, a kilt of course, and a leather belt loaded with all sorts of knives and—an axe! Did everyone in Dornie forget it was the off season and dress up anyway? Of course, she should talk, with her long skirt and cloak.

A few people, also in period dress, gathered about watching them, but it was as if no one dared approach. Well, she reasoned, who wouldn't be reluctant to come near such a man. He was taking this charade pretty seriously. It occurred to her that this could all be one elaborate prank set up by Skye. But then what of Davina? The accident surely would've ended the hoax, wouldn't it? None of this was sinking in, but just to be on the safe side and play along, Harper decided she'd best use her French accent.

She smiled. "Not dead yet. Can you sit up?"

Harper knew she had a limited imagination, but if she could have conjured up the perfect male, this man would absolutely fit the bill. Except, if he were truly a medieval Scottish warrior, shouldn't he be able to sit on a horse better?

He reached his massive hand to her cheek and gently ran his knuckles along her jaw. "Ye are real," he said, his tone one of utter disbelief. "Not an angel."

His touch was like electricity, sharp but oh so pleasant. Forcing herself to examine all this objectively, she shook her head to clear it.

He was asking if she was real? *What about him?* It could be just a pickup line, but if so, she wasn't falling for it. "And no, it didn't hurt when I fell from heaven," she retorted sarcastically. The look on his face was a combination of hurt and bewilderment and she immediately regretted her response. "I'm sorry," she quickly apologized. "I am real." *Are you?* Her skin felt hot and cold at the same time. This new reality warred with logic and Harper had no idea which one to embrace.

Sitting up, he continued to stare at her. "I hae never fallen from me horse before. Certainly nae at the walk." He frowned as if to try understanding what had just happened. Angling his head, he gazed at her in confusion. "Who are ye? Clearly nae a MacKenzie since I would hae remembered ye."

"Nay," she answered in kind. "I am a Forbes. Are ye

badly hurt?" Clearly embarrassed that he had slipped off his mount, Harper didn't want to make it more uncomfortable for him, but she was concerned he had done some damage to himself. The ground was not exactly soft and welcoming.

"Nay, just—it's just ye are so—bonny. And a Forbes. Lucky." There was no guile in his compliment. He closed his eyes and shook his head. "I hae never fallen from me horse," he repeated, said to no one in particular. "Not even in the heat of battle."

It was clearly so disconcerting for him, rather than defensive, as if he truly was puzzled. Harper had to stifle her grin. He sounded so… authentic.

"Thank you—ye for the compliment." Harper was awestruck, but not just by the man himself or by his words. Then, lifting her gaze to the few who had gathered around them, she realized no one was in modern dress. The same question poked at her. Would so many be gathered in medieval clothing if it was the off-season? It would have to be quite the lavish production. But of what? A movie? Maybe. But it all seemed so… real.

Beginning to believe the cloak had worked and she really was in 1562 Scotland was becoming harder to deny. Unless someone was playing an elaborate joke. Maybe she was still asleep. Or drunk? She'd had those two whiskies at dinner. Oh, what the hell. She had no choice but to go with it at the moment. She decided on the real test. "Do ye know my friend Skye?" Quickly, it occurred to her she needed to maintain that French accent.

The man sat up straighter, his surprise and pleasure obvious. "Ye know the lady?"

"Oui." *The lady?* This was really getting strange. "She and I grew up together."

The man stood and, reaching down his hand, he helped Harper to her feet. He towered over her, but his amazing blue eyes and gentle manner suggested she was in no danger. "I am Daimh, and I can take ye to her."

"That would be wonderful." *I'm beginning to think I'd follow you anywhere.* Harper couldn't resist smiling at him. Men from the twenty-first century were never as unguarded as this man seemed.

"I am Harper." Still, it was possible this was some elaborate prank. But that was getting more difficult to deny. Deciding she must identify more than her name, she added, "and a Forbes, as I said before." Hopefully, the Forbes clan was not considered an enemy.

"Good," he said grinning. "Our clans have fought together just recently." Relief flowed through her. One less problem to deal with.

Daimh glanced around for his horse and nodded to a boy in front of a nearby stable.

The boy waved in response and turned away. "Well, it appears me horse has found his own way to his stall. Come, there's a wee boat over here."

"I must get my things." Harper hurried into the cottage. She gathered up the old cloak and gaped at it in awe before folding it away in the satchel.

***

Daimh watched after her as she ducked inside the old cottage. Who was she? Where did she come from? And why would his heart not stop it's pounding?

Her clothes were a bit strange, and her hair was unlike the other lasses, but she was the most bonny lass he had ever laid eyes on. And kind. She hurried to his aid when he fell. He fell! How was that even possible? But one look at her standing there and the world faded to naught and his mind swirled. He had been struck hard in the head before, but even then he ne'er lost his sense of balance. It was as if the faeries themselves had captured his focus, as if they hadn't toyed with him enough. But, unlike before, the sight of this lass gave him a glimpse of heaven itself.

Reappearing at the entry to the cottage, she looked at him in the strangest way, as if she didnae believe he was real either. He'd been frozen in place but for a moment before he finally pushed himself to move forward and take her arm. *Mine, you are mine*, was his only thought. That was ridiculous. He knew nothing of her, not if she was marrit or from whence she had come. But it was as if an irresistible force had hold of him and tethered him to her.

He had learned long ago that some forces could not be fought and trying to do so was only exhausting. But this was one force he would yield to without argument.

***

Returning to Daimh, she followed him to the edge of the loch where a small wooden canoe bobbed in the water, making her hesitate. The vessel was tiny and Daimh was so big, she was afraid he would sink it. Of course, it would be the only way across the water since the bridge wouldn't exist for well over another four hundred years.

As if he read her mind about the fragile craft, he laughed, a sound from deep in his barrel chest. "Stronger than it looks. We will not get wet, ye hae me word."

Stepping into the boat, he managed deftly to stabilize it as he held out his hand to encourage her aboard. She decided she had to trust him. Her pulse thrummed, as if she had too much coffee. This was undeniably exciting, and she'd had so few actual adventures in her life. Unless, of course, this was merely an hallucination.

Once she was seated, he reached down and, grabbing a folded plaid, offered it to her.

Gratefully wrapping it around her shoulders, she hadn't really been aware of shivering until the cloth warmed her. He didn't seem to notice the icy rain, but then he must have been accustomed to it.

As he untied the craft and rowed, she had the chance to admire him more closely and her stomach quivered with little tingles. He was a very attractive man, the kind that had always made her think about the possibility of being swept off her feet. But, with her pragmatic nature, she had always dismissed such nonsense. After her divorce, she had known without a doubt she didn't need a man to make her dreams come true. In fact, men like her ex were the thing of nightmares, nasty and diminishing. But this man, Daimh, was very appealing and this whole experience was already the stuff Skye's fairy tales were made of. No wonder her friend loved those stories.

With little effort, he had them across the water in minutes. He hopped from the boat and tied its rope to a metal post stuck in the ground. Then, he helped her out and, slipping his hand under her elbow, led her up the path to the castle, which rose above them, huge, imposing. There was no doubt it was the same structure she had just visited, but these walls were less dark with age and smoke. With the castle having been built in the 1300s, it was already very old.

This was almost too much to take in and if the man

hadn't had hold of her arm, she might have given in to the weakness in her knees.

"I really can sit a horse," he said, lifting his chin. "I cannae imagine what happened back there, but it was a rarity, I promise."

"I believe you," she said. What else could she say? He was no doubt embarrassed and she knew it would not help his ego if she teased him.

They passed through the gate into a courtyard. Harper couldn't believe her eyes. The surrounding buildings were primitive at best, built of straw and raw timbers and the men, women, children, all dressed in medieval costumes, moved about as if their activities were perfectly normal. Some carried kindling, others piles of fabric. A nearby blacksmith pounded upon a glowing piece of metal upon an anvil. A group of children engaged in a game of chase ran past them, scattering a flock of chickens about Harper and Daimh's legs. And two women carrying baskets of greens greeted them as they neared the main structure. Daimh led her up a flight of stone steps, then through massive wooden entry doors into a huge hall. She's seen none of this on her earlier tour of Eilean Donan.

The floor was covered in woven mats and the sweet scent of herbs and lavender drifted up. The walls were decorated with older tapestries and artwork and weapons. Axes and swords and knives, as well as the horns of deer, attested to hunting as a definite sport here. Or the source of food. A huge fireplace across the hall boasted a roaring blaze and quickly dissipated the chill that had permeated her bones. It was the most perfect of medieval settings. Talk about an imagination—if that was what this was. But she reminded herself she really didn't have much of an imagination. Before now, that is. So then where was the fire-breathing dragon to guard the place? Or was that a different tale?

Her gaze was drawn to a painting on the far-left wall. It was the same one of Skye she had seen on her tour. The colors were brighter but the image was unmistakable. Except now, next to it was the man's portrait Skye had bought at that estate sale. But that wasn't possible. That painting was in Memphis, Tennessee. So how was it here? Unless…?

Before Harper could fully absorb that and all the rest of her surroundings, a whisper of fabric on the stone steps across the room caught her eye and the bark of a dog caused her to start. Transfixed, she watched as the cloth became a gown and then a woman, accompanied by a small black pup, who descended the stairs. Her face was obscured as she concentrated on a piece of parchment.

"Skye?"

Looking up, the woman did a double take, let out a scream of surprise, dropped whatever she'd been reading, and raced down the remaining steps and across the space, sweeping Harper in her embrace.

No, it simply wasn't possible. It was all a figment of her apparently newly discovered overactive imagination. But the woman holding her was solid.

Harper pulled back and gazed into the face of her dearest friend. "Oh my God. Oh my God. Skye? Is it really you? Am I imagining all this?"

Skye was laughing with joy. "Harper! How?"

Daimh must have been reassured Harper was indeed friends with Skye, because he placed Harper's bag at her feet and slipped away.

Skye leaned in and whispered in Harper's ear. "Mon Dieu. Say mon Dieu. I assume you're supposed to be French."

"Yes. Yes. I mean aye. Or oui. Is it real?" Looking around her, she shook her head in total disbelief. She had to be dreaming, but here was her bestie—in the flesh.

"Aye. It is true. You are actually here. But how?" Skye was vibrating with excitement. "Come. Sit over here and tell me all."

The dog let out a yip and Skye bent down to him. "Dionadair, this is my best friend Harper. I have no idea how this has come about, but you must be on your best manners and welcome her."

As if he understood, the little black dog wagged his tail and dipped his head to be petted. A Scottie, of course.

"Good boy." Skye praised him, patted him, and standing, she then took Harper's hand and pulled her to the chairs by the fire, the pup obediently following and lying down at Skye's feet.

Harper was completely nonplussed by everything. Her mouth hung open and it was as if she was in a trance of some kind.

Skye's voice broke through. "I told you it would work."

Harper tilted her head. "But it's not possible."

"But it is. And I am so glad you're here. Ye have no idea how happy I am to see you. Will you stay?"

"Well," she giggled, "I suppose I cannot return to the nunnery."

"What?"

"The short hair. How else could I explain it?"

"You cut your hair! And you actually thought this through. I'm proud of you for thinking outside the box."

"I still don't believe it," Harper affirmed. "I'm just asleep and…"

Skye grinned. "But it is hard to deny."

50

"I suppose." Biting her lower lip, Harper angled her head at Skye. "It really is you and I am really here."

"Yes. So, getting back to your history... we grew up together and you went off to the nunnery? Is that it?" Skye asked.

"Yes, in France obviously. My parents are gone, and my uncle sent me there after my husband died. To the nunnery. But I missed you and could not take my vows, so I tagged along with a priest and his retinue on their way to Mary's court, hoping to find you there. But I heard from the locals the laird...?" Harper hesitated. "Just listen to me. I sound like all that really happened."

"And if you were to tell the truth of how you really got here?"

"Do you think we might be burned as witches?"

"Could happen. If with everything you know as a woman of the twenty-first century... if you are having trouble believing the idea of time travel, what do you think these very superstitious people would think? In a few months, they will pass the Scottish Witchcraft Act and even a hint of suspicion after that could be verra dangerous."

"But still..." Harper heaved a breath. Logic dictated she go along with the fantasy—or was it now the reality? She did trust Skye. If the woman in front of her was undoubtedly her best friend instead of an apparition created by a fevered brain. Harper pressed her fingers into her forehead. It was cool. So much for an illness. "Okay, Fill me in. Tell me what happened after you arrived here. Tell me more about life here. About the laird."

Skye dropped her shoulders with a sigh and a wide grin. "The laird. My husband."

"Wow. I can't believe you actually found him."

"And he is even better than I imagined. Wait until you meet him." Skye was practically swooning. "And now I'm married to him—and pregnant."

"Oh, my God. I mean mon Dieu. I am so happy for you." Harper clasped Skye's hands, her grin so wide it hurt her cheeks. Warmth filled her, knowing Skye's previous life had been one struggle after another. No one deserved a happily-ever-after more.

"I know it's…"

"Unbelievable," Harper finished. Leaning closer to Skye, she whispered, "Does anyone here know the truth of how you got here?"

"Only one. Her name is Neasa, and she runs this place. We were imprisoned together, and I had to tell her. I thought we were going to die, and I wanted someone to know the truth. Plus, she saw my nail polish."

"Your husband doesn't suspect? Wait—you said imprisoned? Like in a dungeon? I don't understand."

"I'll tell you all about it. But a vicious mean girl was responsible." Her lips curled in disgust. "And I'll bet you've met her, since you had the cloak."

"Davina?" Harper asked. "She imprisoned you?"

Skye nodded. "Davina had her eye on Ian and in her jealousy tried to get rid of me."

"How?"

Skye lowered her voice. "It sounds so ridiculous, but the people here believe that potatoes are dangerous. Davina had some brought into the kitchen and accused me of trying to poison everyone. And when I tried to explain they were just delicious food, many of the others were convinced I was trying to hurt them. So they had me sent to the dungeon."

"Oh my God."

"Neasa defended me, so she was locked up with me. Only Freya and Kenna were willing to defy the others, knowing for certain I had been set up. When the men returned, Freya told Ian what had happened, and they rescued us."

"Oh my God. And where was your laird when all this was happening? Where did he return from?"

"He and the others were away fighting for Mary at Corrichie."

"And Davina?"

"She tried to lie her way out of it, but the boy she hired to secure the potatoes confessed after I saved his life and then Davina knew she was doomed. She grabbed my cloak, knowing it was of value but not knowing why, wrapped herself in it and disappeared. It must have been quite a shock to her to wake up hundreds of years in the future."

"So that answers the question of how she got the cloak. But what of the rest? Since there are some big gaps in your story. You said you saved a boy's life. How?"

"I brought doxycycline along with me and it actually cures the plague."

"Plague?" Harper recoiled. "This is seriously getting worse and worse. Go on."

"When Davina sent him to get the potatoes, he came in contact with a French soldier who was ill with it. When Rory got sick, I recognized the symptoms and had Freya give him the antibiotic. And then I had to take some as well, since Davina stabbed me before sending me to the dungeon and the wound got infected."

"Can't leave you alone for a minute," Harper said. Her mouth gaped open as she realized Skye wasn't joking. "She actually stabbed you?"

"She did. And it hurt. But more, it terrified me. I

knew the risk of infection, especially with no way to clean the wound and stuck in a filthy environment. But it turned out fine." Skye smiled. "The course of true love…"

"So it was still worth it?"

"I would do it again in a minute if I knew I would end up with Ian." Taking a deep breath, she gazed off in the distance. "Yes, in a heartbeat."

"I believe you."

Skye turned her focus back to Harper. "Do you know where she is now? Davina? Did you see her?" The worry in her tone was obvious. "And what made you actually believe me enough to come here?"

"Davina is in the hospital in Dornie. In a coma." Harper took a deep breath. "I was worried about you, so I traveled to Scotland to see if I could find you. I stayed at the cottage and was washing my face in the bathroom when a woman—Davina—simply appeared. She was so confused by everything, she ran outside and was hit by a car. She cracked her head and she's now unconscious in the hospital."

Skye's eyes widened at Harper's explanation. "Talk about Karma."

"I was hoping to get some answers from her, but she didn't wake up. But when I went to see her, I checked her clothes. They were clearly not made with a sewing machine and the material was very different from anything I had ever seen."

"So you finally believed?"

Shrugging, Harper grinned. "Not really, but what choice did I have? The evidence was mounting up, so I figured it was worth a try. But, honestly, I didn't think the cloak would work and until I woke up here, I didn't give any credence to any of it."

"Hard to deny now, huh?" Skye smiled. "How does that crow taste? Having to admit my fantasies weren't so crazy, after all?"

"Still, unbelievable," Harper repeated, still reluctant to totally concede. Her gaze wandered across the room, to the table against the wall where Daimh sat watching her with fixed attention. "Who is he?" She licked her lips.

"One of my husband's trusted men. And a kind soul, although he appears very fierce. Most women are afraid of him, so he remains single."

"He's so good-looking." She might even swoon— or not! "Why would they fear him? He can barely sit on a horse."

Skye smiled more broadly. "Well, it doesn't appear you are intimidated. Wait. What? What do you mean he can barely sit on a horse? The man is glued to a saddle when he rides." Skye was clearly confused by this.

"I awoke in the cottage and stepped outside just as he was riding by. Seeing me there, he slipped off the animal he was riding and hit the ground with a thud. It wasn't like I startled his horse. It was at a walk."

Skye laughed out loud. "The thunderbolt. Like in that movie with Cher. "Moonstruck". They talked about the thunderbolt that strikes when you're instantly in love."

"Really? You think I had that effect on him?" Delight surged through in Harper's veins.

"Yes. Daimh rides like he was born on a horse. You must have had quite the effect for him to land on the ground."

Harper's cheeks grew warm with a blush. "Really?" she repeated. All this was hard to accept. Men didn't fall over themselves—or off a horse—when they saw her. He had told her it was out of the ordinary, but she had thought he was just trying to save face. "That's quite the compliment. And from so attractive a man."

"These men with their muscles and bare legs should grace calendars, don't you think? Wait until you see Ian."

"Your husband?"

Skye sighed. "My husband," she affirmed, her expression telling of her love for him.

"You do have it bad. I want to hear all the details of your wedding. Tell me everything."

"See for yourself."

A tall, extremely handsome man had come into the hall and was moving toward them. Harper immediately recognized him from the portrait Skye had discovered at an estate sale. The portrait that had started this whole adventure. The portrait that was in Memphis in present day and yet now hung next to a painting of Skye in the main hall. Harper's mouth gaped open, not for the first time since she woke up. "I don't believe it. It's him!"

"Yummy, huh!" Skye nodded as he approached.

Walking closer to them, Harper could see the love in his eyes as he turned his gaze to Skye. "Is this yer friend? The one ye missed?" he asked, his brogue heavy. Another real Scotsman. Like Daimh.

"Aye. This is Harper. Harper, this is Ian. My husband."

Ian stretched out his hands in welcome. "I am pleased ye are here. Me wife was sad with the holidays approaching to think ye could not join us."

Harper grinned and had to lock her jaw to keep it from dropping even more. He was even better looking in person. "I felt the same," she responded, careful to speak with her acquired French accent. "We have always tried to be together during this time of year."

"Ye came from France?" Ian asked, though it wasn't truly a question. "I couldnae help but notice the accent."

"I was in a nunnery there. But I could not take my vows. My heart wasn't in it, and I wanted to find my friend."

"Well, I will nae tell the priest you escaped the clutches of the church," he teased. "Can ye stay?"

"Of course she must stay," Skye declared.

"Ye are more than welcome." He smiled at his wife and slipped a hand behind each woman's elbow, leading them to the head table that was now being set with platters of food.

Harper turned back to pick up her bag, fearful of letting it out of her sight, then stepped back to Skye and Ian.

He turned his face to Harper. "Come, let us break bread to celebrate your arrival." And then to Skye, "I don't ken this little slip of a lass will eat too much."

Chapter Six

Harper could immediately see why Skye had fallen hard for her dream man. He was not only handsome but seemed kind and intelligent. To say nothing of those legs beneath the kilt. The way these men dressed was enough to make a woman forget everything else.

But then, from what she could tell, all his good qualities were no different than Daimh's. And the others in the clan were so welcoming. Ian's sister, Maisie, was glowing with her pregnancy and her solicitous husband, Errol, hovered over her. Not exactly as Harper had pictured married life in the medieval era. History had proclaimed that during these times men were men and women were lesser beings unworthy of anything but bringing dowries and being brood mares to be ignored until they produced an heir. And then ignored some more. Not the case in this household.

Skye introduced her to Freya and Conall, praising the other woman for saving her life when she was confined to the dungeon. And there was Kenna, who Skye whispered ran the kitchen like a drill sergeant, but always with some kindness beneath the gruff. And last, but not least, was Neasa.

Coming forward, the older woman embraced Harper. "I hae heard much of ye and I am pleased to see

58

ye here. From France, are ye?" She sent a knowing glance to Skye, who looked a bit guilty.

"Ummm, oui."

Skye had said she had told Neasa the truth. Harper was certain if there would be an opportunity to talk to the other woman privately it would prove to be interesting. As shocking as this was for Harper, she could only imagine what a woman in the sixteenth century would think as she learned of the world hundreds of years in the future.

Harper sat next to Skye at the main table, which stretched across the front of the room, as they ate freshly baked bread and rich lamb stew abundant with vegetables, followed by custards and a variation on sugar cookies, clearly courtesy of Skye and her skills in the kitchen.

"Still baking," Harper teased.

"Not so easy with different ingredients, but I still love it. I couldn't just sit around all day."

Harper leaned in close so she wouldn't be overheard. "No soap operas to watch, or bonbons to eat?"

"Not a one."

"This place is so different." Harper peered around the main hall with so many people sitting eating the mid-day meal. "The word of the day. I mean, more than just historical. The atmosphere, the people..." Her gaze lighted on Daimh, who immediately looked up as if sensing her. Smiling, he lowered his head, but not before she noticed he had deep slashes of dimples on either side of his mouth.

Nudging Skye, Harper whispered, "Is he shy?"

"Who?" But her lopsided grin let Harper know Skye was teasing her.

59

"Daimh."

"I don't know. I mean, not with me or Ian, of course, but I think you caught his fancy. And you seem pretty interested."

"Not that I am planning to stay, of course, but I hope so. About catching his fancy, I mean. He is the most attractive man I have ever seen. And no man has ever fallen off so much as a chair for me before. I'm flattered to say the least."

"What ever happened with Jeff?'

"Who?" Harper laughed. "Oh, the one I had a date with when you were leaving? He kind of pales by comparison."

"No doubt," Skye grinned. "I would love nothing more than to see both you and Daimh happy and if that's because you're together, all the better."

"I can't stay here," Harper declared softly.

"If you say so."

***

Daimh couldn't keep his gaze from her. Harper was so bonny. Not only that, but she smiled with gentleness and seemed to have no fear of him. Her cropped hair was no doubt due to time in the nunnery, but it didn't detract from her womanly appearance. Her eyes were a glorious shade of pale blue, like the delicate blossoms that dotted the hillsides at the first breath of spring. And her body was enough to stop all blood going to his brain, even dressed as she was in the ill-fitting clothes which were probably due to the choices at a cloistered place. Just looking at her was enough to make him want to recite poetry. Well almost.

He thought of himself as a strong man, but when she smiled at him, his knees grew weak and his stomach filled with butterflies. It was embarrassing. And when he touched her cheek, his hand burned with tremors. He needed to summon some courage, ask her if he could accompany her on a walk on the morrow. Getting to know her more, perhaps he could learn to control his response to her before he humiliated himself in front of her and the others.

The meal finished, Lady Skye was about to sweep Harper away when Daimh approached them and loudly cleared his throat.

"Daimh?" Lady Skye questioned. "Is there something you require?" He noticed that Harper didn't miss the ill-suppressed smile on her friend's face.

Lowering his gaze, in case he betrayed his nervousness, he cleared his throat again. "I was wondering if the Lady Harper might wish to visit Dornie in the morning and be shown around—since she's new here and all."

Grinning widely, Harper nodded, a lovely blush coloring her cheeks. "I would like that."

Nodding briskly, he stepped away and strutted to the door and on his way to the field to practice and expend some of his energy. He had no wish for his hands to shake when he was trying to impress her on the morrow, and working himself to exhaustion should help.

***

Watching him walk away, Harper shook her head. "He is the cutest mountain of a man, isn't he?"

Skye nodded. "He is. But come, I wish us to catch up out of the hearing of anyone who might not understand."

61

Following Skye up the stairs and into a spacious room filled with sunlight, they sat in front of the fire. The walls were covered in tapestries depicting ancient battles, but their colors had faded with time. Chairs were placed about the space and several embroidery frames were scattered about, the work partially completed. As she sat back in the comfortable seat, Harper drew in a deep breath and her muscles relaxed. The dog called Dionadair was at Skye's heels and obediently sat when they did.

"When did you get a dog?" Harper asked.

Skye reached down and patted the pup. "Oh, he's not really mine. We just took a liking to each other when I arrived. I think Ian was a bit jealous at first, but then I suppose he decided if the dog approved of me I must be all right." She grinned. "So how are you doing?"

"I had no idea how tense I was," she said.

"Not used to traveling through time?" Skye teased.

"Funny."

"So what do you think now?"

Harper heaved a sigh. "I should have been reading more fairy tales growing up. This is too much. In fact, if you weren't sitting here, I would think I had truly and completely lost my mind."

"I understand. I didn't really believe it at first either. It's a lot to take in."

They spent the next few hours catching up. Skye revealed all the details of finding Ian, falling in love (instantly for real) and then struggling to fit in. Telling of the terror of her near death experience in the dungeon brought tears to her eyes, and Harper reached over for a tight hug. "I am so thankful it ended well," Harper said.

"Me, too."

Harper talked about Davina's accident and the

process of actually deciding to try the cloak. "So against everything I believed."

"I'm so proud of you. And so happy you're here!"

"I can't stay."

Skye dropped her gaze, then lifted it again to look Harper directly in the eye. "You said that before. Why not?"

It was not the question Harper expected and she pressed her hands together, thinking about a response.

"Why not?" Skye repeated, interrupting the quiet.

"Because," Harper answered.

"Well, that's not a reason. I'm serious. What do you have that's so important you need to rush back to the twenty-first century? Because for every excuse you give, I'll give you another to stay."

"Work. The hospital needs me."

"Hah! I know you're valued, but no one is irreplaceable."

"Okay, hot showers, hamburgers, makeup."

"Warm baths, grilled meat over an open spit, and who cares about makeup. There are face creams here and the clean air is fantastic for the complexion." Skye struck a pose to emphasize her words.

Harper scrunched up her face in thought. "Medicine, electricity, running water."

"Herbs, candles, and fresh cool water from an unpolluted stream."

"Social media?"

"Don't be ridiculous."

"Okay, how about clan wars, disease, the danger of being accused of witchcraft?" Harper pressed.

"I guess it's always something," Skye teased.

Harper sat back. "You love it here, don't you?"

63

"I do. And to add to the list of reasons for you to remain—Daimh. Where in the future would you ever find a man like that?"

Harper heaved a sigh. "He is pretty delicious. But I don't even know if he really finds me appealing. His attention might just be because I am new."

"Oh, get that miserable ex-husband of yours out of your head. That hideous voice that told you all your flaws. And then humiliated you." Skye shook her head in disgust. "I've seen the way Daimh looks at you and I have no doubt he would love to get to know you better." She wiggled her eyebrows and grinned. "And I still find it hard to believe he actually fell off his horse."

"Really? You think he is attracted to me?"

Skye laughed out loud. "Yes really. I haven't been here that long, but I haven't seen him look at another woman like he looks at you." Skye angled her head. "How about this. The holidays are not so far away, and you and I have always spent them together. Let's maintain that tradition. And, if by Hogmanay you still want to return, I won't try talking you out of it."

"Hogmanay?"

"It's Scots for New Year."

Harper bit her lower lip and pondered this. "Well, my parents won't miss me. I don't even know where they are for a change."

The unspoken was that she never knew where they were. From the time they could foist her off on a nurse or caregiver, they had gone on with their jet-setting ways. Her parents were trust fund wealthy and they always made sure Harper was cared for and set up financially. Money instead of love. In fact, though she would never admit it to Skye, Harper was the one who had bought her friend the ticket to

Scotland, knowing Skye couldn't afford it. Why shouldn't Skye be allowed to follow her dreams, even if Harper had no idea they would turn out to be real?

"I am dying to know what finally convinced you to try the cloak," Skye said. "You—ever the pragmatist."

"Some things are just too much to deny. There were so many clues: Davina appearing, her clothes, but I guess the final thing that convinced me was the portrait of you hanging in the castle. Obviously from the sixteenth century. And no painting of Ian." She shook her head. "I wonder what the people here would think if I told them his portrait would wind up in America hundreds of years in the future."

"I know. Now in a storage unit awaiting my never return." Skye suddenly clapped her hands together and her face lit with her smile. "Really? My portrait is still hanging in the castle. I had hoped it would still be there and if you ever ventured there after I left, seeing it would let you know I was well and happy."

"And there's now a legend to go with it. The woman who appeared suddenly and stole the laird's heart." Harper pressed her lips together. "Maybe I shouldn't tell you this part…"

"What part? You can't do that. Tease me like that."

"Well, apparently you have three children. Two fine sons and a daughter, as the tour guide told us."

"Wow." Skye hugged herself with joy. "Good to know."

"Was it the same painter? Your portrait and Ian's?"

"Yes. Conall. He's very talented and he painted it as an early holiday gift to Ian and me. Which, considering he's about to be married, was amazing."

"And he's marrying…?"

"Freya. Who helped save me from the dungeon."

"You said before that once you were freed and Davina was found to be the culprit, that she grabbed the cloak and disappeared," Harper said. "Was she here in the castle when it happened?"

"Yes."

"Odd, since she re-appeared in the year 2024 at the cottage."

Skye raised an eyebrow. "Interesting, since she was transported from one place and ended up in another, albeit not far. But how did she get across to the loch? And…?"

"What is it?"

"Well, when I received the cloak, the note said it would always return on its own to the place it started."

"Which would have been the cottage, right? If that's the case, how long until it disappears?"

"The note said weeks. It didn't specify how many."

"Did it mention how often it could be used? Do you think it will take me home?" Deep seated anxiety compressed Harper's chest. Could she end up here forever?

"I don't know. But would it be so terrible to have to stay?"

"Skye, I don't belong here. I have a job, a family."

Skye raised an eyebrow. "A family you literally never see. And your job? Do you love it so much?"

Harper huffed a sigh. "I… I don't know. Even if I stay…?"

Skye smiled. "I like that 'even if'. There's no guarantee you can even go back. So, maybe, just to be safe, you should just decide to stay here."

"But, what about Davina? Even if I get back to the present, she may never wake up. She fell pretty hard. But what if she does? And starts talking?"

Skye threw back her head and laughed. "They will lock her up in an institution. Who would believe her?"

Harper shook her head. "Tell you what. I'll agree with what you said earlier and stay through the holidays. That's only a few weeks. Then I can make a decision. And if I do decide to go back, we can see if the cloak works." And if it failed to return her? Would it be so bad to have to remain here? "You are, after all, all the family I really have."

"Deal. And you're my family, too."

They were interrupted by Neasa, who strode into the room with a knowing look. She dipped a quick curtsy and quickly took the chair Skye indicated. Leaning toward Harper, she took a deep breath. "Nae doubt you two have much in common and much to talk aboot. Would ye share some of it?"

Skye nodded to Harper. "It's okay. I told you. She's the only one who knows."

Neasa scooted her chair closer, fairly shivering with excitement. "I want to ken everything. Lady Skye has nae been forthcoming enough on details and it's so unbelievable. And now they are two of ye."

"And no Davina." Skye stated this with undisguised pleasure.

"Aye. But where is she?" Neasa asked.

"She traveled to the future. To my time. And now she's in a coma in a hospital in Dornie," Harper answered. "She was hit by a car. They say she has traumatic brain injury."

"Coma? Hospital? Car?" Neasa's look of bafflement made Harper and Skye giggle.

"A coma is a deep sleep that one doesn't always wake from. A hospital is where they take people who are

67

ill. There are physicians and nurses there who tend them. And a car…?" Looking to Harper for help in this explanation, she was clearly at a loss.

"A car is like a wagon that doesn't require horses," Harper explained.

"Ye tease me. How is that possible? Do they use some other animal?"

"No. It's hard to describe, especially since Skye and I take these things for granted. Just think of a horseless carriage."

Neasa gave them both a side-eyed look, her skepticism obvious. "And the other? Traum…?"

"It means she will probably remember very little and even if she does, no one will believe her. They will think her memories are merely a result of the injury."

"I have heard of such things," Neasa said. "When warriors are struck on the head, sometimes they are nae the same after."

"Exactly. And with no way back here, since I have the cloak, we can rest assured she will not betray us," Harper said. "When I return, I can make certain that she receives no credibility."

"Return?" Skye's face fell. "I wish you'd forget about that and just stay."

"But I am a product of the future," Harper reasoned. "I don't belong here." Did she keep repeating that to convince herself? At least now she was able to admit all of this was actually real. But knowing in your head and accepting it wherever your common sense dwelt were two different things.

"Yes, you do belong here. You will. It will just take a little time."

Harper angled her head in thought. "There are many

things in the future that are not even dreamed of here. I suppose I am spoiled."

"What things?" Neasa prompted.

"Like indoor plumbing, so there is no longer a need for chamber pots and…"

"…candles that light without fire," Skye added. "And so much more. But not necessarily better."

"I would like to see some of these—miracles."

"Well, it's not so wonderful as you might imagine. For every 'miracle' as you call them, there are problems." Harper said.

"See. You're already beginning to see it my way," Skye grinned.

"Me head is already full, and I hae no wish to learn of more problems. I'll leave you to yer catching up. But I think I shall hunger for more details later." Shaking her head as if to assimilate all they had told her, Neasa slipped from the room.

"She told no one?" Harper whispered when Neasa was out of earshot.

"No. When we were in the dungeon, it was certain we would die. And what good would it have done if she had told the others. They would certainly think she had lost her mind. And she doesn't even know about airplanes or computers."

"She loves you," Harper said. "It's clear you bonded. But I suppose when you're facing death…" Harper paled at the thought of her best friend dying.

"And I love her. We would have bonded even if we had not faced the hardship together. She was my first friend here and my most loyal companion. Well, except for Ian, of course. And you."

Harper peered around the space. "I heard the Scots

were a frugal people, so I understand there is not much in the way of furniture. But what there is, it's beautiful. Everything about coming here is a surprise."

Skye grinned. "It only gets better. I promise. After a few days, you'll think the only McDonalds is another clan.

Chapter Seven

Harper woke up in her huge bed under piles of covers. Her dreams had been fraught with visions of being transported to Scotland in the sixteenth century. Blinking awake, realization slowly permeated. It was no dream. Quickly sitting up and looking around, she was convinced she remained in the sixteenth century. She was still here even though it defied everything she believed.

Someone had left a warm woolen robe at the foot of her bed, and she quickly wrapped herself in it. On a small table against the wall, a bowl and pitcher waited, no doubt for washing, a linen square alongside it. Dipping her hands in the icy water, she splashed it on her face. It wasn't a cup of Starbucks, but it did wake her up.

A kind soul had lit a fire and it beckoned cheerily as sunlight spilled in through the windows on her right. On a chair in front of the fire, several gowns and undergarments waited, including a heavy linen shirt and a long skirt made from a plaid. Woolen hose and soft slippers would keep some of the cold at bay and another tartan lay on the chair, apparently to wrap around her shoulders. That and the velvet cloak she had brought with her, with its warm lining, should stop some of her shivering. And off to the side, a small dagger sat in a leather sheath attached to a belt of sorts. Of course, Skye

71

had told her she would need an eating knife since silverware was not plentiful and there was no need to waste coin on such a luxury as forks. A quick look under the bed confirmed her the bag with the magic cloak was safe and still hidden.

A grin curved her mouth as she remembered that she was to go for a walk with Daimh today. Getting to know him would be a totally new experience. How should she act? This was a completely different culture with dissimilar manners and behaviors. She would prompt him to do the talking. Ready for what more adventures await her, she opened her chamber door and walked down the steps to the main hall.

Very few people were around, but a woman serving food noticed her and indicated she should sit at one of the trestle tables. A bowl of what appeared to be steaming oatmeal and some biscuits they called bannocks were placed before her, along with a mug of bitter ale.

She smiled her thanks and took in her surroundings as she ate until Skye exited the kitchen.

"Did ye sleep well," she asked, slipping onto the bench beside her.

"Aye," Harper responded, with no little sarcasm. "I can't get used to the brogue."

"Ha. This is nothing. Wait until you spend time with Daimh and he slips into Gaelic. And yes, ye'll soon learn there are no secrets here." She stifled a laugh. "Well, other than ours, that is."

"Did I hear talk of a wedding?"

"Aye," Skye responded, grinning. "Conall and Freya will stand before the priest in two days' time to speak their vows. I am so happy for them. Did I mention that he had wanted to pursue Davina?"

"Oh my God." She, above all, knew what it was like to be married to someone horrible. Apparently, Conall got lucky and was not to be burdened with that—what did they say here instead of bitch? *Galla*?

"I know. Sometimes men can be so dense. A flash of boob and they're putty."

"What happened to change his mind?"

"Well, I think he was getting hints of Davina's true personality before they left for Corrichie to defend Queen Mary, and he was definitely beginning to notice Freya. When they came home and he realized what Davina had done to Neasa and me, he obviously made the right choice."

"You know, when she first appeared at the cottage, she seemed—I don't know—like something nasty lurked under her surface."

Skye nodded her agreement and before they could continue their conversation, Daimh strode into the hall from outside.

His hair was damp, and Harper wondered how it was possible to bathe in this cold. But, these were the hearty Scots, and she would just have to toughen up if she were to think of staying. The thought unnerved her, but less so than she imagined it would.

"Good morning." His eyes bright and the smile lighting his face warmed her to her toes. "Could I hope ye would still like a tour of the village?"

"Oui. I would love it."

"Have a lovely time," Skye said as she stood and gathered up Harper's plate and hurried back to the kitchen.

Harper stood, slipped her hand around his arm, and he led her out into the courtyard and through the gate. His hard muscles rippled under her fingers and a little thrill of

73

excitement ran up her spine. They angled down the hill to a dock, and he held his arm out to guide her to a seat in a boat. More flutters tickled her insides.

"Nae frightened this time that I'll drown ye?" he teased.

"No. I mean nay. I feel quite safe with ye."

If she was not mistaken, the big man blushed a little.

In minutes they were across the loch. The sky was a steel grey, threatening rain, and Harper hoped it would hold off at least for a while. Anxious to spend time with this glorious man, she didn't want the weather interfering. Unless, of course, they could find a secret cave.

Obviously, the constant threat of a downpour didn't deter the locals from going about their business. Taking Daimh's arm and again reveling in the strength she found there, they walked up to the cottage which had been her point of arrival and Harper hesitated. It was nearly impossible to believe this was the same place that hundreds of years in the future would be a luxurious accommodation. Now, it was a broken-down wreck of disuse and abandonment.

"This is where I first laid eyes upon ye," he said, " and I imagined I was dreaming."

That makes two of us.

"Why did yer escort not bring you directly to the castle?" he asked. "All manner of things can happen to a lass left alone." His disapproval was clear.

Harper had to think quickly. "The priest and the others were in a hurry and since they had been kind enough to bring me this far, I felt it improper to impose by delaying them further."

"Well, luckily, Dornie is a safe village. No one here would dare molest ye, especially knowing of your friendship with the Lady Skye."

Continuing to walk into the village, Harper was amazed at the locals offering their goods. Just like a farmers' market in the present day, people were selling freshly picked winter vegetables. Open-air stalls allowed people to move between the wares. There was a woman with bolts of cloth laid out on a table and another hawking beautiful ribbons of all colors. Eggs, sausages, and other foodstuffs beckoned and Daimh bought some fresh bread and cheese. Tearing off bites, they shared the fare as they walked along, admiring the merchandise.

"It is always like this?" Harper asked. "The merchants and the goods?"

"Nay so much all the time, but more so during this time of year. Although we're forbidden to celebrate Christmas since the Reformation, many still buy gifts for each other to exchange. We just don't call it by name."

"Why?"

"Why what?"

"Why did the Reformation end the celebration of Christmas?"

"A man named John Knox brought it about. Our Parliament merely desired to step away from the Roman Catholic Church and ended up destroying it here. Catholic practices were made illegal, and anyone caught celebrating mass could be put to death. But that didn't change the beliefs in the people's hearts."

So many thoughts went through Harper's mind. Mostly how no matter what point in history you found yourself, someone was always trying to change things, not necessarily for the better.

"Skye said you do celebrate the New Year. Hogmanay is it?"

"Aye, and a glorious party it shall be, as it is every

year. I am hoping you will accompany me, and I may claim a dance or two."

Harper's chest filled with those flutters again and she smiled. "I would be honored, but I fear I am not much of a dancer."

"Forgive me, I did not think. Of course the nunnery would not have had much dancing. Believe it or nay, I can be verra light on me feet."

"There was not so much drinking either," Harper returned, grinning, hoping that was true. Some nunneries produced wine. "For me, that is," she corrected. "But I did sample some whiskey on my way here. I liked it." And a tiny part of her still held out that whiskey was responsible for this hallucination. It was, however, becoming impossible to deny that this was her new reality.

"Well, we can see that you have more, then," Daimh said. "Whiskey, that is."

"Why Daimh, would you take advantage of a wee lass by feeding her spirits?"

He appeared horrified. "Nay. I would nae do such a thing."

Harper patted his arm. "I was but teasing."

Relaxing, he dropped his gaze, then straightened. "But, if ye were willing…" His voice had lowered, as if he were speaking more to himself than to her. Clearing his throat, he lifted his chin. "Tell me of your life in the nunnery. How did ye spend yer days?"

How indeed? "Well, we did the usual nun stuff." Harper could not believe those words had come out of her mouth. Before she could retract them, his bellow of laughter filled the air.

"You jest with me. People, wumman, do not usually

do that. I like it." He pulled her forward. "Come and we will see what the other craftsmen hae brought today."

***

Daimh tried to stop staring at her. He did. But she was so bonny. So different from any of the other lasses he had ever spent time around. Harper was the kind of *baineann* who could steal a man's heart and never let it go. He couldn't decide what it was about her exactly, but from the moment he slipped from his horse, which was inconceivable, he was thunderstruck.

And more than that, he desired her above all others. Wumman were not so hard to come by if he had the need, although he believed that most succumbed not to his charm, which he was certain he lacked, but because he was braw. Warriors, even though they were feared, were seen as a challenge to some lasses, their taste of adventure.

But Harper was so unlike any other. She actually teased him and when she smiled, she could reach into his chest and hold him captive. To be ensnared like that was—terrifying. What if they were to marry and beget a bairn like his brother? It could tear them apart, as it had his mother and da.

When Thomas was born, his da had walked away, blaming his mother, thinking she had provoked the wrath of the fairies. His da was ne'er to return.

Daimh hoped to never make the same decision and leave a child, no matter what the fae had in store for him. But when dealing with the faeries, sometimes their cunning games for amusement dealt mortals terrible consequences. His much older sister, though, had married before their brother was born, so she was unaware of what had befallen their family. But there was no explanation for the curse, so how could he explain it? He just had seen the result. But now his sister had a husband she cared for and three lovely, healthy bairns. That's what Daimh hoped for himself one day, but the secret always held him back. Was marrying a chance he could take? If his sister had escaped the wrath of the fairies, were they saving more mischief for him?

That was his private terror. And why? Why was his family cursed? And was it just his mother and da or him as well? There was no answer he could find.

Today, watching Harper and seeing the marketplace through her eyes was a completely new and exciting experience for him. Many times he had strolled the streets and perused the goods, occasionally spending coin on some necessity or other, but today all he could think of was how he wanted to buy everything that caught her eye just to please her. But again, so unlike others, she seemed to have no desire for him to spend his money on her, seeming happy just to be in his company.

At one point, her toe had caught on an uneven cobblestone, and she stumbled. Quickly, he grabbed her about the waist and brought her aright. His heart pounded and his blood ran hot through his veins as she turned to thank him, her mouth but an inch from his own. That mouth of hers, those lips, so ripe and pink and delicate, so made for kissing. Imagining how they would taste made his manhood react and he quickly angled away so she would not see. The last thing he wished was for her to be scandalized by his bad behavior.

Unfortunately for him, the Pandora's box of desire had been opened and it was all he could do to keep his hands off her and his thoughts on anything else.

When they returned to the boat and he helped her inside it, the wind blew her scent of roses, tickling his nose. Closing his eyes, he prayed for strength to resist all the urges that were clouding his brain. If she knew his secret, she would be repulsed, and he could not abide that. Nor could he take the chance the fae might direct their harm to her because he already cared for her.

***

Returning to the castle, Harper noticed more activity than that morning. Sounds of clanging pots and Kenna calling out directions from the kitchen filled the air and Neasa paused only long enough to flash Harper a smile as she hurried past.

Harper needed to talk to her best friend. She was desperate to sort out her confusion and her feelings for Daimh. When he caught her arm as she nearly fell in the marketplace, it was all she could do to not to pull him closer. Wondering what it would actually feel like to have his mouth on hers so occupied her thoughts afterward, it was difficult to concentrate on anything else. Luckily, the craftsmen were anxious to show their wares and provided a distraction. But the attraction to him had happened so fast. She told herself it had been awhile, and it was probably just lust, but she knew better. She was drawn to this man like an irresistible force. She should not really be surprised. After all, everything to do with this experience was—mystical. There was no other word. Fading into the background was the woman who demanded facts, figures, data. And it was unnerving trying to reconcile what was happening.

Skye strode down the stairs, Freya next to her

vibrating with obvious excitement. Of course, they were preparing for her wedding. It was made special since the laird obviously valued both the bride and groom. According to Skye, Freya had been instrumental in saving her life and Conall had been a loyal friend to the laird since forever.

Freya nodded, grinned, and ran to the main door and out into the courtyard. Skye motioned Harper to join her by the fire.

"Good morning. Thank you for the clothes."

Skye grinned. "I had to hide yours. Close examination would definitely cause suspicion. Clothing here isn't made of polyester and put together with machine stitching. And they were a little out of date."

Harper shrugged and laughed. "I did what I could."

"I get it." They shared a quick laugh.

"Can I help with the wedding preparations?" Harper asked.

"Nay. I will arise early tomorrow to make a cake and Kenna has the women in the kitchen making all manner of stews and meats and vegetables. And Freya created her own gown. She is so talented with a needle and thread. I have to show you the gown she made for my wedding. It's gorgeous."

"I am so sorry I missed it. I always hoped I'd be there to see you happily married. It breaks my heart."

"Me, too. I am so glad you're here now, though."

Harper squeezed Skye's arm. "I still can't believe it." Exhaling, she gazed around the main hall. "Who will come to the wedding?"

"Mostly MacKenzies and MacRaes. The custom is actually for the clans to intermarry to form alliances, but when Ian realized Conall and Freya loved each other, he would not even consider marrying either of them to others outside the immediate clan. In fact, Freya has been in love with Conall for years."

"Weren't lairds supposed to do that as well? Marry outside the clan?" Harper raised an eyebrow in question.

Skye grinned. "Aye. But since I was a Blaine, which is a Scottish clan, and also French," she winked at Harper, "Ian felt certain that the queen would bless his marriage to me."

"That is amazing luck."

"So how was your time with Daimh?"

Feeling the heat rise to her cheeks, Harper dipped her head.

"That good?"

Lifting her gaze skyward, Harper hugged herself. "Skye, he's not like any other man I've ever known. And it's not just that we're in medieval Scotland. He is sweet and kind and so handsome. And such a gentleman. I was hoping he'd kiss me. He did kind of make it clear he wanted to. I was sure it would freak him out if I made the first move, but I managed to behave."

"Good for you." Skye leaned closer and bumped shoulders with Harper. "We don't want him thinking you're a loose woman."

Harper laughed, the sound coming from deep in her throat. "How do I explain I'm no virgin?"

"That's easy. You were married—nothing wrong with that. You could say he died."

Harper hated to be reminded of that time in her life. Finding her ex-husband with another woman, in their house, in their bed, was the most ego devastating experience of her life. Not that Richard had been a particularly good husband, always criticizing her and lecturing. Still, actually seeing his betrayal was nearly overwhelming.

When they were married, Richard had also even gone so far as making Harper's time with Skye impossible. They had to sneak phone calls and lunches and it strained their relationship. When the marriage ended, after two interminable years, Harper could tell that Skye was as happy and relieved as she was.

Would a man like Daimh end up trying to control her? And then tire of her? Seek the company of another? Somehow, she doubted it. He struck her as the kind of man whose honor and loyalty meant everything to him.

But what was she thinking? She needed to go back, or rather forward, and here she was contemplating a relationship with a man in the sixteenth century. Her head was spinning.

Chapter Eight

The wedding was lovely. Priests were hard to come by on the Highlands, especially since the Reformation, but Eilean Donan was a place where men of the cloth knew they would be safe and could perform the duties of their station.

Freya was glowing, her gorgeous blue velvet dress floating about her like a cloud and her face alight with such pleasure, it was a joy to behold. Conall said his vows earnestly and with a look of love that warmed all who witnessed the exchange. When Freya repeated hers, they each lifted a hand, palms together, and Conall wrapped a piece of fabric around their wrists three times. The priest blessed their union, and a cheer went up from the crowd. This was truly a love match. Harper had no doubt they would be happy and produce many children.

After the ceremony, the feast was laid out in the main hall: rabbit, fish, pheasant, stews, vegetables, tarts and pies. In the center of the main table was a magnificent cake. Harper had no idea how Skye had managed it, but it could compete with any bakeries in the future. Decorated with bits of heather, which was not so easy to come by in winter, it was magnificent. The casks of ale and wine flowed and the musicians played both rousing tunes and sweet romantic airs.

Harper found her way through the crowded hall to where Daimh stood. His smile more than suggested he had been waiting for her and it grew ever brighter when she sidled up next to him.

"Ye look bonny," he said.

She nodded her thanks, wanting to return the compliment. He was so handsome, so masculine, so desirable.

The tables were pushed to the walls to make room for dancing. The men lined up facing the women and soon the music began, the tune jaunty and melodic. In a series of turns and crosses, couples linked arms following the rhythm of the music.

Harper watched in fascination. It wasn't long before the steps began to make sense to her. "You said you were light on your feet," she said to Daimh. "Will you show me how it's done?"

"Aye. With pleasure." Taking her hand, he led her out onto the floor. They joined the others and soon Harper was dancing and laughing with abandon. This was so much fun, and the feeling of freedom was exhilarating. Daimh was grinning at her and all she could think was that she wanted to fling herself into his arms and have him hold her.

Finally, completely winded, they separated from the group to rest. Daimh angled his way over to a cask of ale to fetch two mugs, twice looking over his shoulder at her. Never in her life had she felt so appreciated, so beautiful.

Skye had appeared at her side and Harper realized she hadn't heard what her friend was saying.

"What? I'm sorry. What did you say?"

Skye laughed out loud. "If you could take your eyes off Daimh for a moment, perhaps you might have heard me," she teased.

"I can't stay here." Knowing there was so much less conviction in her statement had Harper chewing on her lower lip.

"So you keep saying, Harper. But you never seem to have a valid reason why."

Harper sighed. "I could so fall in love with that man."

"And?"

"And then I suppose I couldn't go back. But—what would I do here? I don't belong."

"Where your heart is, that's where you make your home."

An ache spread across Harper's chest, like bands tightening. Home. Looking around, Harper saw family, loyalty, love, companionship. Harper had never known any of these things, except for Skye, who was here and happy. And then there was Daimh. So strong, so kind, so—okay, admit it… delicious. But seriously, this was the 1500s in a foreign country. Most of the people spoke Gaelic, the most confusing tongue she could ever imagine. Or with a brogue so heavy she had to strain to understand the words.

Some languages had always come easy. Any with a base in Latin were merely logical extensions and easy to understand. But Gaelic? No way. Of course, she knew if she applied herself she could manage, but—but why was she trying to talk herself into remaining here? She was so confused.

***

The older woman slowly opened the door of the wee cottage and gave Daimh a crooked smile, stepping aside

85

to allow him to enter. He scanned the small room and braced himself as the boy threw himself into Daimh's waiting arms. Thomas was no longer a wee lad and Daimh had feared he would never make it beyond a few years. Even though he was switched by the fairies when he was born, he was turning into the sweetest and most loving of children. The bairn's almond shaped eyes and small hands and feet distinguished him from other lads his age. But Daimh could not have loved Thomas more. Sometimes, he did wonder what the fairies did with his real brother; he hoped the lad was happy wherever he was.

When Thomas was born, Daimh's mother was convinced the bairn was a changeling and that the fairies switched the boy with her own as a punishment for she knew not what, or mayhap it was one of their tricks for their amusement. But his mother nurtured him, hoping if she kept him well and safe, the fairies might relent and return her true son. His da just up and left, disgusted with the changeling child, and after two years, when the bairn was weaned, his mother just gave up hope and took to her bed, never to rise again.

Caring for the babe fell to Daimh, who was nearly seventeen. He could not let the fragile little one waste away. He found Eilidh who agreed, for the right amount of coin, to care for Thomas, and the widow woman had minded his brother ever since. And kept the secret of his existence.

Eilidh did not fear the wrath of the fairies; her cottage was filled with charms and herbs. And Daimh was certain she had grown to love his younger brother as much as he did. Eilidh's own daughter, Iona, had also been widowed a few years ago and eventually returned to live with her mother and she seemed willing to care for

Thomas as well. Neither shared the secret. Together, the women were able to carefully hide the bairn and since their cottage was at the edge of the wood in Dornie, they managed to keep to themselves.

Daimh hoped Iona would be blessed with another husband and children one day, since she was still young, but she rarely left the cottage unless she was working at the castle. When he had told her she needed to spend more time among the clan in order to find her future, she would just smile at him and say she was both patient and content. She had told Daimh on many occasions that no other women would be as happy to accept Thomas as she was.

Knowing that many might wish the bairn harm and almost all would reject him, Daimh, a warrior, had sworn to protect this child, and other than the two women, he intended to make certain no one else ever discovered the truth. With one exception. He had decided to tell Ian in case something was to happen to him because he knew Ian would protect the child. But other than that, he told no one. He had never even told his sister. He did not wish her to bear the burden of the secret or have to worry about her own family.

If that meant he would never marry, so be it.

Perhaps his real brother would be returned to him one day, but after so many years, he doubted it. And if that were to happen, he knew he would miss sweet Thomas.

Thoughts of Harper swirled in his mind, and he fervently wished he could hope for a future with her.

The idea of keeping Thomas a secret for the rest of his life preyed on him. If something were to befall him, Eilidh or Iona would continue to care for him, or Ian would step in. He ached to be able to confide in someone like Harper. But what lass in her right mind would willingly tie herself to a man whose mother and da had been cursed? It was possible the fae did not intend for him to be punished, but one never knew with them. Since he and his sister were not changelings, it was possible the sprites were satisfied. Was it a chance a *baineann* would take?

The image of Harper's lovely face, her brilliant green eyes and her lush curves permeated his imagination. Heading to the training field, he knew his only hope was to pound out his frustrations in practice.

***

"How does anyone possibly learn Gaelic?" Harper spoke out loud to herself as she watched some of the women putting food on the trestle tables for the mid-day meal and speaking the odd language among themselves.

"Ye start with the simple phrases."

Quickly turning, she found herself nearly pressed against Daimh's muscled chest. She hadn't realized he had come up behind her. Her heart skipped a beat before pounding against her ribs.

Protectively, his arms had wrapped about her, making her feel safe and warm and incredibly excited, all at the same time. Snickers from some of the other women made Harper take a step back, her embarrassment obvious.

Clearing her throat, she smiled. "There are no simple phrases in Gaelic," she responded.

"*Tha mi gad larraidh*," he whispered, leaning so close she could feel his warm breath on the shell of her ear. *I want you.*

"Which means?"

He shook his head. "Another time and place," he answered.

"It means another time and place?" She was confused, more so when he laughed out loud.

"Nay. It means I will tell ye what it means another day."

"That's not fair. How can I learn if you don't tell me? I could be saying anything when I speak it and never know until... well, who knows what could happen."

"Aye. How about *mas e ur toil e,*" he said. "It means please."

"Masher toilda?"

Laughing again, the sound warming her to her inner core, he nodded. "Close enough."

"Teach me another."

"*Tapadh leibh.*"

"Tapa leeb?" she repeated.

"Aye. It means thank ye."

"I shall practice, but I fear it is a long way to being fluent."

"That ye wish to try is enough." The look he gave her was scorching. It was clear he had other things on his mind beside linguistics. Her breasts tightened at the thought of his touch, and she pressed her lips together to control the urge to stand on her toes and kiss his mouth. But, of course, only loose women did that, and she was supposed to be a lady.

"Will ye take another walk with me this afternoon?" The look in his eyes was so full of hope she nearly laughed out loud.

"I would be honored."

A grin split his face and she marveled at his straight white teeth. Definitely something she wouldn't have expected, but then so much about him was a surprise. Noticing a scar along his jawline on the left side, she couldn't resist boldly reaching up and touching it. He reacted as if he'd been struck by lightning.

Quickly pulling her hand back, she pressed her fingers into her lips. "Forgive me. I just wondered how you got that scar?"

Gently grasping her wrist, he placed a kiss on the soft underside, and she suddenly understood his reaction. She felt it, too.

Taking a moment and inhaling, he finally answered her. "It was at Inverness. Just a scratch."

"Does it hurt?"

"Nay. It was… yer touch."

It was not a scratch that left such a mark, but then this was not a man who gave into injuries or pain easily. Harper imagined he must be magnificent in a fight, just like in the movies. But here, it would not be play-acting, and the cost would be in real flesh and blood. The thought made her shiver. And so had his proclamation her touch affected him.

Harper had never experienced anything like this before. She's read about it, heard stories from newlyweds in the blush of new love, but she never believed it was possible. And yet, when this man was near her and she could feel the heat of him, all she could think was she wanted to have him, wanted him to make love to her, wanted to claim him and have him claim her.

"Until later then." He left her and she felt the loss of him. What was she going to do? She was falling hard for a warrior in the sixteenth century. Ridiculous. She couldn't stay here. Could she?

The mid-day meal was served, and Harper was again amazed at how delicious the fare was. She had imagined cheese and bread, but the savory stews and fruit tarts were incredibly delicious. She had better find some activity to burn calories before she gained huge amounts of weight. Skye on the other hand… Her friend was eating as if she thought someone would pull the food out of her mouth and Ian was laughing at her. But she had a valid excuse, which made Harper fill with joy for her friend.

"Are ye eating for two or ten," he teased her.

"You will regret that remark when your son appears. I need to see to his nourishment."

"Are you planning for him to spring full grown then from the womb?"

When Skye looked as if her feelings were truly hurt, he reached over and hugged her. "I but joke with ye, *mo ghradh*. You have ne'er been more bonny and it makes me happy to see ye eat when so many wumman can keep nothing down the first months."

"I'm fat," she complained.

Harper burst out laughing. "We should all be so fat. Ian's right, you are glowing."

"Truly?" she asked around her pout.

Ian and Harper exchanged a look, and he gave her a slight nod. "I shall ne'er again make such unthinking comments."

Harper was certain he would spend a great deal of time making up to her for the thoughtless remarks. How wonderful. When Richard, Harper's ex, insulted her, he never apologized. He always thought it was his place to correct her and dominate. This was a different world in so many ways.

Harper glanced over at Daimh who sat at a table against the wall. Wishing he could sit beside her, she knew there were specific rules as to who sat where. Unless you were directly related to the laird, ye did not sit at his table. But she missed Daimh's nearness. This meal could not end soon enough for her, for she was anxious to go on that walk with him. Lots of walks. A good way to maintain her weight. But she imagined other forms of exercise she might like to try as well.

The thought was new. She had never desired a man as she did Daimh. She would have to control herself.

***

Watching her eat was pure torture. Those full lips, rosy and aching to be kissed. The way she ran her tongue along the bottom. His imagination took flight. His gaze drifting down, he took in her full breasts peeking out from the neckline of her shirt. Her breasts were full and so nicely filled out the top, playing a peeking game above the fabric. Imagining how her ivory skin would feel under his fingers made all the blood flow downward and he shifted in his seat.

Wishing he could inhale her scent and savor her nearness wasn't helping. He dare not stand lest he embarrass himself. Harper was so desirable he wondered why he hadn't already had to fight for her. It had not escaped his attention that others in the hall noticed her, but happily, she seemed to be looking his way when she smiled.

Think of other things, he silently admonished himself. *Like sharpening his sword.* By the faeries, that only made it worse. Trying to direct his thoughts was futile. He could only think of her and possessing her, claiming her as his own.

Pondering what the Lady Skye would think of a match between her friend and himself filled him with dread. What if Skye didnae approve? What if Ian told her his secret? Nay, the laird would never do that. He had sworn to never reveal what he knew, and Ian was an honorable man. But that didnae mean he would be happy about Daimh claiming his wife's closest friend.

Knowing Ian loved him as a brother and trusted him helped some of his concern. But he had to think of his brother. If the secret were to get out, the lad would certainly be banished or worse. It was the way of things. Most bairns who had been switched did not survive, the fear of the fae so great. But Daimh could not accept that fate for Thomas. And was it so much to ask that he protect his brother?

Conflict swirling in his brain made him dizzy. He would fight three men at a time or storm a castle without a second thought. But thinking of bedding or wedding this amazing lass had him at a loss.

The only consolation was the plan to spend time with her this afternoon. At the very least, he could be in her company for a time. Would this meal ne'er end?

Chapter Nine

Snow swirled through the air and the wind shoved its way between the edges of her cloak, so Harper was delighted to be able to lean into Daimh.

"Do I keep you from your tasks?" she asked.

"Aye, but without sorrow. It willnae hurt to take a few hours away from training. And I enjoy your company, lass."

They had taken a small boat to Dornie and now walked along a stream, listening to the gusts as they encouraged the bare limbs on the trees to dance in gentle rhythm.

"Tell me of yer life before ye came here," Daimh suggested.

Here was Harper's chance to tell him she was no longer a virgin, even though speaking of Richard was never something she enjoyed.

"I was married to a cold and brutal man who did not treat me well."

Feeling Daimh stiffen, nostrils flaring, and growling in anger. It was very gratifying. From his reaction, she was quite certain it would never occur to him to abuse a woman. "How long did you suffer him?" he asked, his tone clipped.

"Two years that seemed like twenty."

"How did it end? If he still lives, I would be pleased to see to his apology." His tone left no doubt as to how he would achieve that.

"I discovered he had a mistress and set me aside for her without remorse. But he was not as happy as I was. And then I was told he died." Not exactly a lie. Richard was certainly not alive now.

"And ye entered the nunnery."

Harper had to make certain to keep her story straight. "Yes. My mother and da were gone and my uncle thought it best."

"Then ye have no dowry? Yer husband didnae return it when he no longer claimed ye?"

Harper had to think fast. "My uncle controls it what was left of it, but since I had no suitors, I did not worry about it." Pressing her lips together, she searched her mind for details. "My uncle does not know I left the nunnery, and I am not concerned that he will look for me. I am safe here with Skye until the time comes I must go back."

He stiffened beside her again and frowned with displeasure. Harper angled her head in question. "Have I said something to offend you?"

"Nay. It's the thought of ye leaving here. It is most… unpleasant."

Thrilled that he wanted her to stay, Harper pressed against him tighter. "'Tis cold," she said as her excuse.

Undoing the plaid wrapped about his shoulders, he placed it over hers.

"That feels nice," she responded, though she preferred the heat of his body. She had to remember she was a lady in the sixteenth century and shouldn't be entertaining carnal thoughts. But his scent on the cloth

95

smelled of leather and smoke and man, making it difficult to keep her mind out of the gutter.

Suddenly, he placed a finger up to his mouth indicating she should be quiet. Narrowing her eyes, she wondered what he had heard. Instead of speaking, he motioned for her to wait where she was while he searched for the source of the sound.

He took hold of her arm and pulled her toward the trees and braced her back against a large trunk, ensuring she was not visible. Then, she watched him melt into the landscape. Now she was wary and feeling woefully unprepared for this danger. She held the plaid tighter around her as the hair on the nape of her neck rose. Trepid, she searched the foliage for Daimh, but he had disappeared. Where did he go?

Hearing a branch snap, she peeked around the tree to investigate, taking a step forward. Was Daimh just pretending to tease her? But something told her there was danger and she tried to move back behind the tree, but it was too late. Three men surrounded her and she cried out in abject terror, her limbs shaking with fear.

They hemmed her in and were so close, their stench was overwhelming. She had to breathe through her mouth to keep from gagging. Knives rested in their hands, glinting in the sunlight and promising death. Where was Daimh? her mind screamed. She couldn't believe he would desert her.

"Well, well, lookie what we have here," the largest of the men said. By how the other two deferred to him, he seemed to be the one in charge. "I'll have a turn and ye two can hae what's left. That is, if she doesnae want another go with me." His heinous cackle laden with depravity revealed rotten, crooked teeth.

He tweaked her chin and Harper recoiled at his putrid breath, swallowing back the rising bile in her throat.

"That not be fair. Ye got to go first on the last one and she was dead before we had a turn."

"Maybe this one likes it rough, eh lass?"

Pure raw terror had her frozen to her core and she prayed they had not attacked Daimh before they appeared here. If they had hurt him, he couldn't help her. And the vision of something bad happening to him made her ache.

The wicked leader reached out and grabbed the top of her bodice, yanking her to him. Petrified, she swung at him, beating his chest and head to the laughter of his companions.

"Tulloch Ard" reverberated in the air. Harper didn't have to guess it was the MacKenzie war cry as an enraged Daimh flew out from the trees like an avenging angel of death. The men turned away from her, their attention on the warrior who threatened. Stepping further back from her attackers, she watched in abject terror as Daimh swung his claymore and his axe, one in each hand, cutting two of the men down before they could even react. The stench of blood filled the air as the third man, who had acted as leader, pulled his own weapon, and faced Daimh.

Snarling, he swung his sword and Daimh twisted away as the weight of the miscreant's steel pulled the attacker off balance. But he quickly recovered and met Daimh blade to blade.

Harper couldn't stand by and just do nothing. What if Daimh needed help? What if she needed to protect herself? Scurrying to the nearest dead man, she snapped up his dirk. Fearing she might be more of an obstacle than a help, she hung back, ready if she was needed. Her breath

97

came in panicked gasps as she watched the two square off. She had never been so frightened. Her pulse was pounding so loud it deafened the sounds of the battle.

Gripping the blade by the hilt, she waited for a possible opening to aid Daimh, but he moved like a dancer in a duel with the devil. She was having trouble assimilating that this was actually happening before her eyes.

A slash, a feint, a deflect. The two were evenly matched in size, but Daimh seemed much more in control. His block became a chop, his parry a riposte. His face showed no expression, his focus complete. The opponent swung out of pure frustration and missed. The move proved to be a fatal mistake. Daimh's claymore found its mark, nearly cutting the man in half across his midsection. The man, shock upon his dirty face, dropped to his knees, the sword slipping from his hand. He crumpled over and an icy cloud expelled from his mouth with his last breath.

Her adrenaline flowed through her at a fever pitch. This was real. So very real. Her body could have been violated, her life taken. Daimh could have been murdered before her eyes. The weight of it was all too much. Her knees weak and throat tight, she leaned back against the tree to steady herself.

With no other threats to eliminate, Daimh turned his frantic gaze to Harper. Blood splattered his clothes, but, thankfully, he was unharmed. Relief washed over her as tears coursed down her cheeks.

He wiped his weapons on the last dead man's tunic and quickly tucked his claymore into the sheath strapped to his back and his axe into his belt, before racing to her. He swept her up in his arms and held tight. Never in her life had she felt so shaken, so safe, so excited, so stunned by what had just transpired.

His mouth came crashing down on hers with a ferocity that took her breath away. His tongue pressed between her lips and danced with her own. He kissed her mouth, her cheeks, her neck, the sensitive place below her ear, his breath hot. The primal impulse drove her to madness. Slipping his arm under her legs as her knees failed her, he carried her away from the dead men down to the bank of the burn, where he laid her gently on the moss.

Hesitating, he seemed to wait for a sign from her. The visceral heat and intensity of near death drove her to madness. There was no need to doubt or think more of it. She wanted him, needed him to quell the agony of desire and make him hers. She reached for him and wove her hands in his shoulder-length hair, pulling him closer. Then his hands were everywhere. As he cupped her breast under the plaid, Harper moaned with pleasure. Nothing had ever felt this delicious. That is, until his lips replaced his hands. Had she died and gone to heaven? This was what the poets wrote about. And she wanted more.

He wrapped them both in the plaid to keep out the chill wind but didn't slow his sensuous assault on her yielding body. His lips worshipped her nipples, then slid down her abdomen until his fingers and his mouth teased and toyed with her most sensitive parts. Wanting him inside her as she had never wanted a man before, she lifted her hips and wrapped her legs around his waist. The passion and adrenaline combined. He thrust himself deep, pulled back, and thrust again. Crying out in the sheer sensations that flooded her, she exploded in a shower of stars, gasping for more even as she soared on the waves of the first release.

Growling with lust, he pumped in and out as she was re-ignited and together they rode the heights of their climaxes.

Exhausted, her limbs like melted butter, she pulled him against her, holding onto the feeling of oneness and utter joy.

Lifting on one elbow to ease his weight off her, she wrapped herself tighter about him, letting him know wordlessly that his body was a comfort rather than a burden. Their breaths mingled in the afternoon chill, keeping each other warm and safe from the intrusion of the world.

Finally, he eased over onto his side and stroked her cheek. "I hae ne'er been so frightened, lass. When I heard them approach, I circled around to get behind them for the advantage. But I realize now I left ye more vulnerable and I can only ask yer forgiveness."

Puzzled, Harper angled her head. "I did wonder why you disappeared for a moment. But it was my own fault. I was curious. If I had stayed where you put me, I would have been hidden. But you saved us. Were you as frightened as I was?"

His laugh vibrated against her. "Nay, I had no fear for meself. I only worried they might harm ye and then death would not be sufficient for them."

Blinking at this revelation, Harper was speechless. This man, this warrior in her arms, just faced three vicious attackers and his only concern was for her safety. He seemed to care nothing for his own. No man she had ever met would sacrifice himself to protect her. If this wasn't love, it was certainly the stirring and she reached to bring his body closer.

He kissed her again, more gently this time, but no less enticing. With agonizing slowness, he ran his hands up and down her body. This time, their lovemaking was slow and tender, and Harper was lifted into what felt like another plane of existence. She had never dreamed it could be like this and the thought terrified her. This was a man who could break down her defenses and touch her soul. How ironic that she had to go back hundreds of years to find him. But the question remained—how could she ever go back now?

***

She must think me a barbarian. First she watched me cut down three miscreants who threatened her. And then, like a starving animal, I ravished her. Not once, but twice.

The woman was so full of passion, he thought he might hae died and gone to heaven. Her skin was like the finest velvet, her mouth a harbor for his tongue, and her body pure magnificence. She welcomed him as a long-lost soul aching for a haven. Oh, to nestle in that sanctuary forever.

Just the thought of what had transpired had his cock hard again. He would ne'er be able to get enough of this lass even if he bedded her every day, twice or thrice a day, for the remainder of his life. He had known she was perfect, sent to him as if by the faeries to make up for every hardship he had ever suffered in his life. But he also recognized it as the cruel prank that it was. He could ne'er have her as his bride, ne'er confide his secret, for she would certainly reject him if she knew. What lass in her right mind would choose a man who was the target of the wee folk? If only he knew why the fae were angry. And again, the thought came. What if they were nae mad at him, but at his mother or da? Then he would nae be at risk.

So it might be possible, that the faeries were done

with playing tricks on him and Harper was meant to be his. Was it possible? But there was still the matter of his changeling brother, a truth she could ne'er accept and one he could not abandon, no matter the reason. 'Twas the thing of torment. Then again, maybe she was stronger and braver than he imagined and a possible fae curse would not send her running away.

***

Harper gazed upon Daimh as he rowed them back to the castle in the small boat. Not only was he devastatingly handsome, but so brave and honorable. The splotches of blood on his tunic did not offend her and she realized they were a sign that he would protect her at all costs. And he was an amazing lover, too. Everything she had ever dreamed of and more.

"Thank you. For protecting me."

"Nay, lass, ye ne'er have to thank me for that. It is me duty. And me honor."

"Who were they?" she asked.

Shrugging, he shook his head. "There are men who have no clan loyalty and simply roam about, looking for anyone they can rob or…" He didn't finish the sentence.

A warmth like liquid honey filled her. This man was the stuff of fairy tales and all she could ever want in a partner. But there was that question again. Could she stay here? Could she live her life in so foreign a place? It made no sense, but then, matters of the heart rarely did. Isn't that what the poets said?

***

When they returned to the castle entrance, Daimh kissed her cheek and said he hoped to see her later. After he took his leave to attend to duties, Harper entered the hall.

Maisie and Freya ran up to her, trilling with excitement. "The queen is coming for a visit!"

"The queen? Mary? Queen of Scots?" Harper responded.

The two women nodded, vibrating with glee. Harper noticed Skye following behind them, the color drained from her cheeks. The twittering girl left to spread the news and Skye approached her, took her hands, and pulled her toward an alcove. She peered over her shoulder to make certain the others would not hear them.

Harper could read Skye's mind and knew her trepidations. If the Queen did not believe their stories, they could be labeled spies or witches and hanged. The thought was horrifying.

"It will be okay. We got this," Harper reassured her, hoping she sounded convincing, but she was as frightened as Skye looked.

"We'll be exposed," Skye whispered.

"No. We are smarter than that. You know history. I have traveled in France and can remember locations. And we both speak French." She hesitated but pushed away the growing anxiety. "How much time do we have?"

"The messenger said a sennight."

At Harper's confused look, Skye managed a smile. "Seven days. But one miss-step, one mistake, and we are both doomed."

"We got this," Harper said, hoping for the truth of her reassurance.

The two turned back to the other women, pasting smiles on their faces.

"So exciting," Skye said aloud so the others could hear. Neasa had just joined them from the kitchens and placed a hand on Skye's shoulder. "It is manageable, my lady. And we will not disgrace ourselves, or put ye at risk. Ye have me word," she whispered. And she swept away to see to the myriad of chores.

"That thought never crossed me mind," Skye responded to Neasa's retreating back. Looking at Harper, she forced another smile. "We will have time to get our stories straight."

Harper heaved a sigh. "In the meantime, how can I help prepare?"

"If you could help Neasa supervise the cleaning and airing of chambers…?"

"Thank you. It will be nice to have a purpose. And later, we will plan."

They were, indeed, busy. The queen was coming to visit, and the work was frantic. The floors were swept and sprinkled with fresh mats made of rushes intermingled with lavender and rosemary. Linens were scrubbed and the kitchen was a flurry of activity. Everything had to be perfect.

Days passed and Harper barely had time to even speak to Daimh. They would exchange a smile or a brief touch as they passed in the hall, but Harper wanted to spend time with him. Their lovemaking was an epiphany and Harper wanted to reassure herself this was all real. How ironic, to determine what was actually true when she was living hundreds of years in the past.

Four days had gone by, and the work went on from sunrise to sunset. But the sense of excitement permeated, and no one seemed to mind the additional efforts. After all, their queen was honoring them as their guest and there could be nothing more wonderful.

Harper was carrying an armload of sheets through the main hall when Daimh approached her. Just the nearness of him quickened her heart.

"I want to apologize." He pulled her into a dark corner so they would not be overheard.

"Apologize?" Did he believe their lovemaking was a mistake? Her stomach tightened at the thought.

"I took advantage of ye, lass. My blood was hot and all I could think was how those villains could have hurt ye and it blocked me good sense."

Harper did not want any misunderstanding. "Do you regret it?" she asked, fearful of his answer.

A slow smile lit his face. "Nay. Never. But do ye?"

"Nay. In fact, I would not mind trying again. Without the attack first, that is." Heat rose to her cheeks. Would it put him off that she was so bold?

His mouth dropped open in surprise. "Do ye mean it? Because I can think of naught but ye and how much I want ye."

Relief poured through her. "The castle quiets by midnight and all are exhausted from the extra work. And my chamber offers privacy." Was she again too forward? After all, this was not the twenty-first century. Here, woman needed to behave a certain way. That is, unless they were to be thought of as whores.

Skye was approaching, so Daimh gave Harper a quick nod and was gone. It was hard to miss Skye's raised eyebrows. "Find a friend, did ye?" she asked, her sarcasm obvious.

Harper tried not to feel embarrassed. Skye was, after all, her best friend in the world and Harper knew Skye would be happy if she was happy.

"We need to go for a walk and plan," Skye said,

pulling Harper's thoughts from Daimh and the coming of midnight. "Time is getting short."

"You're right," Harper agreed. "We need to have our stories straight."

"I have been giving it some thought, and I am certain we can do this." Skye's usual confidence had returned, so Harper relaxed.

Once outside, they wrapped their cloaks tight against the chill wind blowing from the loch and walked far enough from the castle walls to ensure they were not overheard.

"Do you ever get used to the cold and damp?" Harper asked.

"Caen," Skye said, ignoring Harper's question. "It is a relatively small village west of Paris and just south of the English Channel. There are two abbeys there, along with a castle, built in the eleventh century by William the Conqueror and used as part of his power base. One of the abbeys was his, the other built for his wife, Mathilde. In fact, she is buried there, at the Abbey of Sainte-Trinite."

"I think I actually visited there once when I was young, but I remember little of it. And Mary will certainly know of this place." Concern edged Harper's tone. "What if we make a mistake? We could miss details."

"Yes, she might know of it, but I would be surprised if she is intimately acquainted with the nuns or the residents of the area. I can't imagine she would have actually been there. So, it is familiar enough to be believable, but not so much that we will be caught in a lie."

"Did you tell people here you were of the nobility?"

"I did," Skye said. "I said my mother was of noble birth and my father Scottish, but that wouldn't necessarily

106

mean they had wealth. And hopefully the queen will be too busy to pry into details."

"We need more, just in case. And you know the stakes. If we are caught in even one small lie. And your husband would not be able to help you or me."

"You're right. I will say our fathers both worked for the church in Caen as scribes. In fact, they went to Caen to work for the church. And my mother was descended from the Girard family. A distant relative, but still titled. You and I grew up together and…?"

"And I was briefly married. My parents were dead by then and when my husband set me aside, my uncle sent me to the church to become a nun."

"And since my parents were dead, as well, I sought to serve the queen when I was intercepted by miscreants. My guard was routed and I ran and ended up here."

Harper was quiet for a moment, digesting all this. "I would believe it," Harper laughed.

"Let's hope everyone else does. But it sounds good."

"Thank heaven for your studies in history."

"We should go back and help. There is still much to do to prepare for a royal visit. But—how is Daimh?"

Harper heaved a sigh. "Amazing. I've never met anyone like him."

"And you're not likely to again if you return to the twenty-first century." Skye grinned. "Besides, you'd miss me too much."

"I would," Harper agreed.

Chapter Ten

Waiting had never been one of Harper's virtues and as the hour grew later, worry clutched at her. With no clocks, she had to guess the time, but she was certain it had to be near midnight. Stepping to the window, she looked up to see the moon high in the sky. Yes, definitely midnight.

Maybe he would not appear. Maybe he *did* regret being with her. Maybe she wasn't good enough. "Stop it!" she admonished herself out loud. She could hear Skye in her head and knowing what her friend would say. "That's your ex talking. Banish him!"

A noise caught her attention. Was that a tap at the door? She hurried over to it and, taking a deep breath to calm her racing heart, Harper cracked it open to peer out into the hall. Daimh stood there, actually looking as nervous as a small child caught in the act of doing something he knew was wrong. Harper stifled a laugh and swung the door wide, ushering him inside, then leaning back against the closed door.

Neither spoke for a moment. Then, he slowly drifted toward her, his gaze never leaving hers. Like two magnets, they were drawn together. His hands wrapped themselves in her hair, holding her head as his mouth crashed down, plundering hers, demanding, seeking, exploring.

Responding in kind, she had never wanted anything

in her life as much as she wanted to feel this man's naked skin against her, his body becoming a part of her own.

She quickly stripped her night shift away. Daimh reached for his own clothing when she stopped him. She wanted to look at him, somewhere deep in her soul hoping he would think her as desirable as she found him. She needed to know. And she desperately wanted this to last, to become a memory embedded in her heart, in her body and bones.

With aching slowness, she released his belt and unwrapped his plaid, holding his gaze as they dropped to the floor. His manhood stood erect against her thigh beneath the hem of his linen shirt, evidence of her effect on him, and she inhaled with joy. Lifting the shirt over his head and throwing it aside, her hands stroked his cheeks, his neck, his thickly muscled chest. Her fingers absorbed the feel of him as they slipped behind to cup his shoulders, his back, his buttocks.

He was perfect. His torso broad, tapering to narrow hips, dark hair sprinkled on his chest and trailed down to his manhood. Scars stood out in vivid relief against his sun-darkened skin, and she ached for the pain they must have caused him.

She moved her palms over his hips to his shoulders, then back again, finally curling a hand around his hard shaft. Using a single finger, she stroked the length of it, then slipped her finger between her lips to wet it and resume her attention to him.

***

His breath came in short gasps as he stood motionless while the lass tortured him. His cock was so hard, he thought it might explode, but he concentrated to control it so this would go on. He was no untried lad, but never in his life had he ever experienced anything like this. He craved her, needing to do to her what she was doing to him. He would get the chance. He just had to endure the most exquisite pleasure of his life.

When she dropped to her knees and her mouth, hot, wet, surrounded his manhood, he nearly died with the intensity of it. But he could stand no more. Pulling back, he lifted her and his heart nearly broke when he saw her expression. It was if she had disappointed him, and he wished her dead husband was in the room now so he could beat him to death. Instinctively, he knew the man had made her feel less than she was and Daimh wanted him to suffer for it.

He smiled at her. "That was the most—there are no words. You are simply magnificent," he breathed. "It is merely my turn."

Feeling her relax, he lifted her and carried her to the bed. And touched and tasted every part of her. He cupped her breasts, holding and kissing each in turn until her rosy nipples hardened and seemed to reach for more attention. His lips and tongue eased down to her stomach, her thighs.

Moaning, she lifted her hips, begging for him to enter her, but he wanted to give her climax after climax this night.

Easing her legs apart, she gasped as his mouth toyed with the nub tucked in her secret space, savoring it as it tightened, and she writhed with each touch of the tip of his tongue. She was delicious, like springtime and earth and flowers and the taste of utter happiness.

When he felt her spasm and she cried out, he moved

his body over her and slipped his hard manhood inside her cocoon. Glorious sensations had him fighting to make it last, but she pulled him in deeper with her legs about his waist. Another climax gripped her, and he could restrain himself no more. White hot explosions erupted in his body as his release took him to heights he had never dreamed of before.

Finally, both sated, he was careful to rest his weight on his elbows to keep from crushing her, but she pulled him closer.

"You will not hurt me," she whispered.

Those words, they had more than one meaning. The thought of marrying her and making her his own filled him with sadness, since he could make no promises. He could never share the truth of his secret, but he also knew deep in his bones, he could never let this woman go. She had bewitched him, and he was so tangled in the snare, he would never be free of it. The cords that bound him were silken and sweet and he had no desire to break them. His inner turmoil was tearing him apart, but he had no answer.

***

The castle was ready for the arrival of the queen. Beautiful gowns had been made for the women, with embroidery and golden and silver threads. They had helped each other with elaborate coiffures and then praised each other for their beauty. Everyone wanted to look their very best. And it was time.

Mary, Queen of Scots, was escorted by her retinue into the hall. All bowed or curtsied as she was led to the main table, her chair set apart.

Harper was awestruck. This was one of the most

111

famous monarchs in history and even knowing she would make terrible decisions and end up with her head in the executioner's basket, it was nonetheless amazing to actually see her in the flesh.

The woman was not a disappointment. In fact, she embodied every story about her Harper had ever heard. Young though she was, she was every bit a queen. Tall, beautiful, and graceful, her auburn hair caught the late morning light and set off her pale skin. This was someone born to be a queen and she was breathtaking. No wonder so many fought for her. And even when she had chosen love and religious devotion over good sense, Harper could understand her people's loyalty.

Guards took up their stance behind her as the women brought platter after platter of specially prepared food. There was fish in cream, beef in a rich stew with vegetables, roasted fowl, loaves of fresh, fragrant bread. There were cakes and tarts and candied fruits. The queen ate daintily and praised the dishes and the women who had worked so hard were delighted. The warriors of the clan spent more time gawking than eating, but the food was soon consumed. The conversation was of recent battles and the bravery of the clansmen. Mary spoke of her desire to visit each of her loyal clans to express her gratitude for their defense of her.

After the sumptuous meal, the tables were cleared away against the walls with the exception of the dais and Mary requested the laird and his wife join her for conversation. Ian and Skye were delighted to oblige. After the usual pleasantries, Mary made a point to thank Ian and his clan again for their service to her and inquired if there were any problems she needed to address. The clans were at peace, which pleased Mary. She spoke in elegant French and Harper had never been so relieved to have taken those language classes in college.

Talk then turned to Skye. Mary was very interested in her history and Skye related the story she and Harper had agreed upon.

"It was happenstance that brought you here instead of our court?" Mary asked Skye.

"Yes, your majesty. As I said, I was planning to petition to enter your service, but I was waylaid. And although serving you would have been my greatest privilege, I cannot say I am sorry to have met my husband and now carry another bairn to serve Scotland."

Mary laughed, a sweet melodic sound. "Between you and the laird's sister, Maisie, we do not have to worry about the growth of Clan MacKenzie." Sobering, she sat back. "But the remainder of your family are gone?"

"Aye, your majesty. I have only my childhood friend remaining who has found her way here." She waved an arm toward Harper who stood against a nearby wall. She was afraid there was no avoiding an introduction to the queen, but fear that she might say something that would make Mary suspicious worried her.

"Well, although we are sad that you are not in our retinue, we understand that love is always to be honored. And it appears you have made a good life for yourself here."

Patting her stomach, Skye grinned. "Aye, your majesty."

Mary's smile lit her features. "Then we shall say prayers for continued health and happiness."

The queen then turned her attention to Harper. "It is our understanding your friend has come from France as well. Was it true she was in a nunnery before traveling here?"

Harper was then brought up to be introduced to the queen. It was so incredibly surreal. How was this even possible? She was nervous and very excited. Not only that, but knowing how history had been made, she again worried that she might slip and say something suspect, or anything that could alter history's outcome. Harper took an instant liking to the queen and wished she could warn Mary of her future. But if the course of events didn't play out as they were destined, Elizabeth I might have her reign threatened and that would change virtually everything in the modern world.

Still in awe of meeting the queen, Harper bent into a deep curtsy, glancing over to Skye for moral support. "Your Majesty." It was like being in a Renaissance play with all the characters playing their parts. But knowing it was actually history unfolding and she was an active participant was hard to take in.

Mary indicated Harper should rise and then smiled at her. "You and the Lady Skye are both Scottish bred and French raised. Caen, we were told? A place of rich history. We wish all could appreciate the comfort of our religion. But alas, even the celebration of Christmas is banned here now in favor of the Protestants. It truly saddens us."

***

Three days passed quickly with the feasting and entertainments, but the nights dragged for Harper. With all the additional guards sleeping in the main hall, she knew Daimh dare not sneak up into her room for he would surely be discovered. And Mary might not be pleased with such behavior. But Harper missed him. And, from the hot looks he gave her during meals, she was certain he missed her as well.

Once Mary left the castle and life had returned to normal, Harper anxiously awaited a message from Daimh to let her know he planned to join her tonight. Aching for his nearness, she had to control her desire to just throw herself at him. Not knowing how long she would stay here made her want to squeeze out every moment with the man, since she was well aware she would never meet another like him in the future.

Moonlight wrapped itself around the room as if waiting, as she was, for something to happen. Harper paced the floor. She would not sleep unless Daimh knocked at her door.

No sooner had the thought passed through her mind than she heard a tapping at the door. Rushing to the door, she swung it open. Her warrior, as she now thought of him, stood grinning at her and he slipped inside quickly before he was seen.

"Forgive me, but I could not rest until I touched you again," he said. "These last days hae seemed like an eternity."

Rather than answer him with words, she threw herself into his arms and kissed him with all the passion built up over days. Immediately, he responded in kind and swept her up in his arms, carrying her to the bed.

They made love once, twice, three glorious times, and finally sated for the moment, they both drifted off into a cocoon of sleep.

Harper was vaguely aware that sometime in the night, Daimh slipped from the room, leaving her to console herself with the scent of him which still lingered. She dreamt of a wedding, children, things she thought she

115

would never again consider after her divorce. But, reluctantly, she realized she was wildly and unashamedly in love with the man who had just left her bed. Of course, that was ridiculous. She had known him for such a short time, but then the definition of time was an entirely new concept.

He was fearful of compromising her reputation, which he could solve by committing to her. But then what? He could not travel to the future or could she really stay here? Her practical side debated the pros and cons and Harper had to admit the pros of staying far exceeded the cons of leaving. There was really nothing to go back for. Her life had been her job and her friend, Skye, and little else. And Skye was here.

She could never tell Daimh the truth about her origins. Marriage needed to be based on trust and if they were to marry, she would begin theirs with a lie. A lie she would have to maintain throughout their lives. If she confided in him, he would think her a witch or insane. And then Skye would be at risk as well.

She decided she would have to discuss this with Skye, ask her how she maintained the subterfuge. So, did the end justify the means? It was hard to deny that she was completely—what was the medieval word? Besotted.

Snuggling down into the covers, she closed her eyes and tried to sleep.

***

Sunlight streamed in through the beveled glass, casting rainbows across the bed. If Harper believed in auspices, this would certainly be one.

She had managed to drift off at some point and she

was wondering what the day would hold when Skye burst into the room.

"Get up, you lazy thing. We have work to do," she announced.

Suspicious, Harper frowned. "Work?"

"Aye. Baskets won't fill themselves."

"Baskets?"

"Just because we are no longer allowed to actually celebrate Christmas doesn't mean we shouldn't give out gifts. So, we are to fill baskets for the villagers and deliver them. Come on, get dressed."

Harper was washed and gowned in record time and hurried down the steps to the main hall. Skye, Neasa, Freya, Maisie, and Kenna, along with other clanswomen were already busy sorting tarts and meat pies and cookies, along with handmade dolls and small wooden swords. There were also woolen scarves and gloves and hats.

Standing back for a moment and watching the flurry of activity, Harper asked how she could help. Neasa explained how each basket was to be filled with the toys and other gifts, and then the food on top.

"Where did all this come from?" she asked.

"The women of the clan knit the scarves and things and make the dolls all year long and the men carve the swords for the boys. And then we bake."

"And we get to deliver these things?" Talk about the spirit of Christmas. This was a heartwarming way to spread joy and Harper was thrilled. It also kept her thoughts on things other than her dilemma with Daimh.

"Aye. That is the best part. To see the happiness. It truly is what this holiday is all aboot no matter that the John Knoxes of the world try to convince us otherwise." This from Neasa.

117

After watching for a moment, Harper gathered a basket and began filling it. The women were all smiling and talking about who made what and who should get which doll. The room was filled with such joy that Harper's chest expanded. This camaraderie with other women was something she had never experienced before, and it was wonderful. In fact, everything about being here was becoming more and more fantastic.

After several hours, they were ready to head to the village. Boats were loaded with the gifts and there were several carts waiting for them on the other side of the loch, along with many of the men on horseback. Once the baskets were transferred, the women jumped aboard the various conveyances and headed in different directions. Skye sat with Harper on her cart and they leaned into each other, silently sharing how amazing these people were, how wonderful this experience. The wind whipped around them, the drizzle dampened their clothes, but none of that mattered as they bumped along the rutted roads.

Stopping at each cottage, people ran out to greet them, the children laughing and squealing with delight. Harper hugged as many as she could before it was time to move to the next place. The phrase "giving is better than receiving" was never truer than this day.

***

Daimh was following the cart with Harper, and he was amazed at how comfortable she was with the villagers and their children. She actually seemed to love hugging them and watching their delight as they received the offerings. Boys were already mock fighting with their toy swords while the girls tightly held the homemade dolls to themselves and showed them around to each other. Scarves were wrapped around necks and gloves donned, and it was glorious. Those from the castle were offered cups of ale and cider, but the true warming came from the people themselves. Their singing and dancing, despite the dampening weather, expressed their gratitude. It was impossible not to feel the contagious joy.

Daimh loved this time of year. Sharing bounty and holiday pleasure filled his spirit and crept into the dark places, filling them with light. His only regret was not being able to share this with his brother. Eilidh knew to hide the boy from visitors and Daimh could only imagine the child's heartbreak at not being allowed to join the festivities. Daimh hoped that one day his real brother would be returned and he could share all this with him, too. But he would miss Thomas. Would it be possible to have them both? In the meantime, he dared not allow Thomas to be discovered for fear the people would reject him out of fear.

As he watched Harper, the thought of her learning the truth sent what could only be terror through his body. He feared no man, no war, no fight, but the idea that she would find out about Thomas chilled him to the bone. If she knew, she would certainly think Daimh cursed and walk away, leaving him desolate. But he couldn't continue being with her without revealing the truth. It was not honest and it was not fair.

Seeing her with the village children today, a kernel of hope formed. She obviously liked the bairns, even the dirty ones, and maybe she could accept that Thomas was not his fault. Could she forgive him for the curse his parents suffered? Or would she believe him to carry the curse as well? The thoughts tortured him. Admitting to himself he had fallen in love with Harper and wished to make her his was all that he hoped for. But unless she knew about Thomas, it couldn't be.

***

It was dusk when they headed back to the loch for the trip across. They were wet and cold, but no one seemed to notice. Many of the villagers followed them and were welcomed into the castle for a feast prepared for them and the festivities continued.

After they had eaten their fill, the children gathered around Daimh.

"Tell us a story. Tell us a story." The children's voices rang through the hall and the adults smiled. The meal had been cleared away and the bairns pleas were joined by their mothers and fathers, who were clearly anxious to hear a story as well.

Harper turned to Skye in question.

"Daimh is a wonderful storyteller," Skye responded. "Wait and see."

Daimh nodded and a roar of affirmation filled the hall. He took his place in front of the fireplace, and all gathered around.

"Shall it be the Otter King or the Seal Maidens?" he asked.

"The Seal Maidens," many called out.

"But it has a sad ending," he warned.

"The Seal Maidens," the crowd repeated.

Daimh shrugged his agreement and sat in one of the larger chairs.

"In days long past, those who sailed here believed that our island was home to mermaids, also known as the selkies. In order to turn into humans, though, they had to cast off their sealskins. But they dare not lose them, as the skins had the power to return them to their real form and allow them back into the sea. If, however, the skin was lost, the selkie was doomed to stay in human form until the skin could be recovered."

Taking a breath, he built the suspense like a master.

Harper scanned the faces of his audience, impressed how Daimh held them all rapt with his tale and his voice. If she had not fallen for him before, this alone would eliminate any question. Like the others, she was on the edge of her seat.

"Now, it was well-known that if a human found the sealskin, he could hold the maiden captive." He paused for effect, and everyone seemed to lean forward as one. "One night, three brothers went fishing in the loch. Yes, our loch. They saw three seal maidens frolicking about in the moonlight, having shed their skins, and taken on human form. Well, of course, the brothers were enchanted.

"The brothers quickly gathered up the seal skins, hoping the legends were true and they could make the beautiful wumman their wives. The youngest of the brothers, though, had a soft heart, and was moved to return his chosen beloved's seal skin. As a reward from the seal king, he was permitted to see her every ninth night and if ye watch very closely from a distance away, since ye dare not disturb their meetings, ye can see the lovers reunite when the moon is bright. But you must be verra careful or they will disappear."

"Tell us of the others," a child called out.

"Aye, they were not so lucky." He stopped and frowned deeply at the sons' misfortune. "The middle

121

son's wife found her fur and was able to return to the sea. She loved her husband, but she more missed her home. The verra sad brother mourned until he died, for no other would suit him as wife." Taking a deep breath again, he continued. "But it was true tragedy that struck the eldest son. He did not want to risk his wife leaving him, so he tried to burn her fur in order to prevent such a thing from happening. But he accidently burned her in the process. She screamed in agony at the pain, which was only matched by that of her broken heart. Then he, like his brother, spent the rest of his life in sadness."

Tale ended, the hall grew quiet, until one of the children called out. "Tell us another."

Several voices joined the first, but Daimh shook his head. "I fear it is time for you bairns to sleep, but another time I will tell you of the "Otter King", but only if ye behave and do what your mother and da tell you."

The group slowly gathered blankets and found places to sleep.

Daimh wove his way through the families bedding down to Harper, who stood along the wall with Skye. He was intercepted by a young woman holding a mug for him. Nodding his thanks, he drank deeply and handed the vessel back to her. She was an attractive girl, if a little coarse-featured, and her bosom was nearly spilling over the top of her too-tight bodice. She managed to stroke his arm before walking away with hips a-swinging.

"Who is that?" Harper asked Skye, the green-eyed monster taking a bite.

"Oh, that's Iona. She's a widow who works here at the castle and lives in Dornie with her mother. But don't worry. Daimh has never given her a second glance."

"I wasn't worried," Harper stated a little to firmly.

"Yeah, okay. If you say so," Skye teased.

"That tale was amazing," Harper greeted Daimh as he reached her. "You are a born storyteller."

Smiling in pleasure at the compliment, he took her arm and, nodding to Skye, led Harper away from the others. "May I see you tonight?" His voice was low so as not to be overheard.

"Yes." She hoped midnight would hurry. A warrior, a magnificent lover, a grand weaver of tales. No, she could never leave.

Chapter Eleven

The following morning, Harper and Skye rowed over to Dornie to spend some time alone to talk. Harper really needed her friend and asked if they could seek privacy. But concern for another attack kept them close to the town.

"I believe the queen was convinced," Skye stated as they walked along the edge of the loch.

"I think you're right. At least she didn't try to have us burned at the stake."

"So not funny," Skye responded.

Harper supposed not since it was a real concern.

"What did you want to talk to me about? Good news, I hope."

Before Harper could respond, she caught sight of Daimh on the other side of the narrow woods. His horse was burdened with a heavy basket tied to the back of the saddle.

"Where's he going?" Harper asked.

"I have no idea. I thought we delivered all the gifts. Wait, I believe there is a cottage further back in the wood that belongs to Eilidh. Now that I am thinking on it, I don't remember she had turned out to greet us yesterday. Let's see if we can follow him without being seen."

Slipping between the trees, they watched as Daimh approached a small cottage well hidden, smoke from its peat fire curling above the roof. Knocking, he waited until an older woman opened the door. Handing her the basket, he said something and then behind her, the girl Iona appeared, grinned, and stepped aside to let him enter.

"Iona?" Harper said, the green-eyed monster rising again and turning her tone hard.

Skye smiled. "I have no doubt the basket is for Eilidh, her mother. Daimh makes certain that many of the widows have sufficient to eat and checks on them."

"But if her daughter lives there, why should she need Daimh? I could understand if she was alone…"

"She was alone for years, until Iona returned. It may just be habit. And mayhap there was a reason she didn't appear with the others, and he worried about her."

Harper shook her head. "I have seen the way Iona looks at him. Like he's a roast and she is starving."

"Stop. I am convinced he has no interest in her. Have you seen the way he looks at you?"

"I guess I am just being silly. I just like him—so much."

Skye raised her eyebrows. "So will you stay?"

The same question. Harper's doubts would creep up on her at the strangest times, like just before she drifted off to sleep or in her dreams.

"I dearly want to, Skye, but I have no function here. I have no domestic skills. I can't cook or sew. Maisie oversees the weaving, Freya the sewing, Kenna the kitchen, and Neasa everything else. You bake amazing things. I will lose my mind with nothing to do all day. And there's the matter of the lie. I can't tell him the truth. How do you manage the secret."

"I am certain we can find something you can help with. So many things that require your special talents."

"Like?"

"You are a master of organization. And that is always important. And you are the best friend I ever had. And that is the most important of all." Skye sucked in a deep breath. "Does this mean you'll stay?" Hope was clear in her voice.

Quelling any remaining doubts, Harper nodded. "I have been thinking about it. And you're right. I don't have anything to go back to. You're here and I think I could get used to this life." Harper took a deep breath and blew it out. "But you haven't answered me about the time travel thing."

"I am madly and completely in love with my husband. If he lived in modern times, in another country, I would not have hesitated to travel to him. I just think of it that way. Instead of miles, I traveled years. And what would it serve to tell him the truth. Keeping it from him does no harm, does it?"

"I suppose you're right. And I imagine I could think of it in the same way. Because I cannot imagine living the rest of my life without you—or him."

Throwing her arms around Harper, Skye whooped with joy. "Well, I suggest we get you some more clothes."

"Shopping? Works for me," Harper giggled. "But…" and she groaned loudly, " I don't know. It just goes against everything I believe. The whole time travel thing. And I'm going to have to learn Gaelic." That was followed by another groan, which elicited a laugh from Skye.

"And ask Daimh about his visit to Eilidh. I know he will ease your mind."

***

Afternoon brought rolling thunder and the darkening sky encouraged all to hurry to shelter. Thunderstorms in Scotland in December were not unusual, and no one relished the thought of getting caught in a torrent of icy rain.

The sun had completely disappeared behind thickening clouds. Harper and Neasa had taken a few minutes to walk along the loch and get better acquainted when the blackened sky warned them to take cover. Wind pushed at them, reminding them not to dawdle, and they had just lifted their skirts to make a run for the castle when a slash of lightning lit the sky, illuminating the landscape in an eerie glow. Immediately there was the sound of a blood-curdling scream near the edge of the loch. Freya was keening as if her heart had been torn from her, and beside her, on the ground, was Conall, sprawled wide and appearing lifeless. Beside him, the earth was scorched.

Racing to him, it was obvious what had just happened. He had been struck by lightning. Rain poured over them as they reached a panicked Freya, gripping her new husband's hand to her chest and rocking back and forth, keening in misery.

Running on adrenaline and instinct, Harper fell to her knees beside the prone man and began chest compressions. With no other thoughts than to keep going, no matter how tiring this promised to be, Harper counted, paused, then resumed pressing on his chest. Her entire focus was on making this man's heart resume beating, knowing this was the only thing that could save him. Despite the cold and dripping water soaking her, Harper's body roared with the heat of determination and her sweat mingled with the rain pouring into her eyes. Shaking off the wet drops, she kept pumping and praying—for his life, for the strength to not stop no matter what.

Freya, still hysterical, screamed louder, and tried to push Harper aside, but Neasa restrained her as Harper worked to save Conall. Neasa seemed to understand Harper might have knowledge from the future that could aid the man.

After what seemed like forever, Conall gasped and his eyelids flung wide open. He was alive!

Exhilarated and exhausted by her efforts, Harper sat back on her heels and tried to calm her own gasping. Exhilaration exploded in her chest. She had just saved a man's life. Clasping her shaking hands together, she inhaled with unabashed pride. She had always wanted to be a doctor, but with no encouragement from anyone, she had let the dream fade. How she wished she had been more dedicated. This feeling was like nothing she had ever experienced.

"Oh my Lord, oh my Lord," Freya cried. Kneeling beside him and stroking his cheek to assure herself he was truly alive, she laughed out loud. "You're nae dead."

Yes, Harper re-affirmed to herself. He was indeed nae dead.

"Nae yet," he responded, his breath coming in quick puffs. Smiling tentatively, he reached for her hand and brought it to his mouth for a kiss. "But I feel like I was trampled by a horse."

It was then Harper became aware that a crowd had formed around them, seemingly unaware of the pouring rain soaking them all. "Can we get him inside?" she asked, her tone more of a command than a request.

Several of the men surrounded him and lifted him up, carrying him to the shelter of the castle.

As Harper, Neasa and Freya made their way behind the men, Freya turned to Harper, clearly confused but grateful. "I do nae understand. He was dead and you brought him back to life. How is that possible?"

"He was only sleeping from the shock. The wind was knocked out of him, is all," Harper answered. "I just reminded him to breathe."

Harper and Neasa exchanged a look. It was clear no one here had any idea about CPR and Harper would have to find a way to better explain it. But for now, Conall was alive and probably had a new fern-like tattoo on his skin as a permanent reminder of his encounter.

Leaning in, Neasa whispered, "Can ye teach me that? I ne'er saw anything the like."

Chuckling, Harper nodded. "Absolutely."

Conall was laid out on one of the trestle tables in the main hall and Harper moved to him and touched his neck, feeling for his pulse. Strong and regular. Sitting up, he reached for her hand. "What happened? Freya said ye brought me back from the dead."

As Harper began explaining by repeating what she had told the others, Freya threw her arms around Harper's neck. "Ye saved him. I do nae know where ye learned such a trick, but I was certain he was gone. No one ever survives a lightning strike."

"It is a simple thing, really. I learned it at the hos… convent. But he should rest. He's had quite a—shock." She couldn't resist. Then, exhaling her relief, she turned to go to her room.

"She's a witch!" Iona hissed, her voice echoing through the hall. "He was dead. I saw it. She used an incantation and brought him back from the dead. And now he will be possessed by the devil." She stepped closer to Conall and pointed. "Look at his neck. He bears the sign of the devil."

The telltale fern-like tattoo from the strike was clearly visible on his skin now.

Harper merely shook her head. "That always happens when one is struck by lightning. It is…" She couldn't think how to explain the power of electricity to these superstitious people.

"It is the mark of the strike," Skye jumped in, appearing behind Harper and putting her arm around Harper's shoulders. "I have nae doubt ye have all seen it before, haven't' ye? But it is usually after life has left the body." She looked about the room for affirmation. Several of the clan nodded, accepting her words, but many still looked skeptical. Rage flushed her cheeks. "Ye think because Harper knew a way to save him, you should call her names, and especially something so despicable as a witch." This last was directed at Iona. "You should all be ashamed."

Freya stepped forward. "Instead of blaming Harper and insulting her, ye should all be happy she has healing powers." Freya moved close to Conall. "Do ye feel as if the devil has possessed you?"

"Nay. I feel blessed but verra sore. I will be eternally grateful for Harper seeing to the sparing of me life."

"There, ye see. This was no different than when I sew a wound. Do ye all think that is of the devil?" Freya demanded.

"When you do, it does nae leave a mark," Iona spat.

"And what exactly do ye think a scar is," Freya responded in anger.

Iona took a step toward Freya. "I'm nae saying anything the others aren't thinking."

Revelation came and Harper raised her hands, palms out. "When you get a cramp, you rub it. Right?" Many nodded. "Well, the heart is a muscle, just like in your legs or arms. When Conall was hit with the lightning, his heart did just that. It cramped. I rubbed it and it went back to beating normally again." Harper heaved a sigh. "No magic, no witchcraft. Just pressing on a muscle to make it work again."

The clan members seemed satisfied with Harper's explanation and slowly dispersed, going about their business while Freya helped Conall to their chamber. Looking over her shoulder, Freya's gaze met Harper's. "Thank ye," she mouthed.

Alone in the hall, Skye stepped up to Harper and hugged her. "No good deed goes unpunished, right?"

Harper pulled back, full of concern. "But what if— what if he was supposed to die and I changed history?"

"I can't answer that. Much too metaphysical. But you know you did the right thing. You couldn't let him die." Skye angled her head. "And maybe you saving his life was as it was meant to be."

"But do you think the others listened to Iona and believe that I'm a witch?" Shivers ran up her spine. If the clan believed she practiced dark arts, her life would be at risk.

"No. I think they accepted your explanation. Just don't light any black candles or whisper incantations," Skye teased.

"Very funny." Harper ran her hand through her still soaked hair. "Saving lives is hard work."

"Speaking of work, I have an idea. You ran a hospital, right?"

"I did," Harper affirmed.

"Well, Neasa has always been the healer here, with Freya stitching wounds. But we have no formal set-up.

131

How about if we ask Ian if we can set up a kind of infirmary? That way, you and the others can work together if someone is sick or injured. And, it gives you a purpose and a reason to stay."

Harper pressed her lips together, thinking, then nodded. "It makes sense. But we don't have any drugs."

"Neasa knows all about herbs and things. I used all the antibiotics I brought already, but you can certainly organize what we do have and make healing a more efficient business."

"I don't want to step on Neasa's toes."

"I bet she'll be delighted to have some help. The woman is tireless, but even she can't do everything all the time."

Harper nodded. The idea of being able to impart healing to these people was amazing, a dream come true. "Let's talk to her."

"Then you'll really stay?"

Harper blew out her breath. "I'm definitely leaning in that direction." In her heart, the decision had been made, but she was still reluctant to commit it to words. A tiny kernel of disbelief still lingered. After all, she laughed inwardly, time travel wasn't possible, was it?

Skye let out a whoop and threw her arms around her friend. "I am so happy."

"What if things don't work out with Daimh? And there's still the matter of Davina," Harper said.

"Ah, Davina. Can you imagine if she actually wakes up and tells people she's from the sixteenth century? What do you think will happen?"

Harper thought about that for a moment and laughed. "The psych ward. You're right. I think we'll be fine on that front."

132

"And Daimh sees nothing but you. You must know that."

"Iona?"

"Just because another woman likes him—that worries you?"

Harper nodded. "You're right. I've never been a quitter."

"Then don't start now."

Chapter Twelve

Harper had never taken the time to watch the sunrise. Her life had been one of work and responsibility and practicality and such frivolity as standing and watching the sun warm the sky from deep blue-gray to pink and orange and pale azure was a revelation.

Standing just outside the castle walls, she gazed above her at the wisps of clouds, their underbellies dark with more promised rain, and she inhaled. No smog, no beeping horns, no sirens cutting through the quiet. She had only been here a short time and already her priorities were softening at the edges. The frantic was replaced by a sense of peace, but also of purpose.

She did have a place here and a magnificent man she was beginning to have real feelings for. And he was obviously attracted to her. Knowing she needed to fight the impulse to control everything, she recognized she needed to apply the skills she had to help these wonderful people.

Even without any real formal training, she retained things from simply being in the hospital environment. Like CPR. Like basic hygiene.

Life here was so very different. It was definitely more simple in some ways, with daily survival a part of the everyday. Her thoughts drifted to the time she had spent with Daimh. After the attack in the woods, she had decided it might not be a bad idea to learn how to defend herself in case she was ever caught again without protection. And she knew that same warrior was the one to teach her what she needed to know.

Arms wrapped around her, and she instantly knew who warmed her back. Turning, she smiled up into Daimh's handsome face and reveled in his touch.

"Will you teach me to defend myself?" she asked, and nearly giggled at his reaction.

"From me, lass?"

"No. Of course not. But what if I happen to be away from the castle and…"

He inhaled deeply, his nostrils flaring. "Aye. I hope I will always be there to defend ye, but ye are right. Ye should ken how to wield a blade." It was clear the thought of her having to fight was distressing to him, but he nodded. He indicated the small eating knife at her waist. "I do nae think that would be a verra effective weapon unless your meal attacks ye," he grinned, teasing. "So, aye, I will see to it you learn some skills. After the midday meal, come to the training field and I'll show ye some ways to protect yerself."

***

Watching her come across the field, her hips swaying and her smile just for him, made his heart soar. This was ripping him apart since he knew he could nae ever walk away from her. He needed to declare it to the world, to make her his. But what about Thomas?

He had kept the secret so long, with only the laird and the widow and her Iona being his confidantes, it was difficult to imagine sharing the secret with another. But if there was any hope of a future, he had to tell Harper the truth. And risk all. Thomas was a huge part of his life. He could never turn his back on his brother, or rather the changeling that had taken his brother's place. He had grown to love the lad and he would never be able to walk away. What if Harper could nae accept him? He supposed he had to find out the truth if he hoped for any more with her. If Thomas was a problem for her, then it would tell him all he needed to know about the lass. But in his heart, he was certain she would love the child as much as he did.

"Are you ready to show me how to become a mighty warrior like yourself?" Harper asked, standing on her toes to kiss his cheek.

"Aye, my brave wee fighter. By the end of today ye shall be as good as I, even though it hae taken me years to learn my skills," he said, winking at her.

Harper threw her shoulders back, her chin in the air, and stood straight. "Then I am ready."

Daimh pulled a handsome dirk from his belt and held it out to her, hilt first. There was a lovely carving of a wolf in the wood and the blade, clearly sharp, caught the mid-day sun.

Reaching for it, Harper was surprised when he pulled it back. "Ne'er take this for granted, lass. It is not just a pretty piece of work. It can do great harm and save ye, so it is worthy of respect."

Nodding, she sobered and again reached for the weapon, examining it carefully. Over the course of the next hours, she learned how to hold it properly, how to strike with it, how to conceal it.

He retrieved a leather belt with a sheath for the dagger from his sporran, tied it around her waist next to the girdle holding her eating knife, and slipped the blade into the casing.

He patted it and raised his gaze to her. "Do ye feel better now?"

"I do. I will never be the warrior you are, but I believe that just having this weapon and knowing how to use it makes me stronger."

"Good. I plan that ye should never be unprotected, but it ne'er hurts to have yer own defense."

"Will you come to my room later?" she asked.

"Aye," he grinned. "There is something I wish to speak to ye aboot."

Her cheery expression faded to worry. "Is there something wrong?"

"Nay. Just a matter we should talk aboot."

"Daimh… is… is there another in your life?" Harper looked as if asking the words was uncomfortable, painful even.

"Another? Another lass ye mean?"

At her nod, he smiled as he took a step toward her. "There has never been anyone like ye and the fact that ye like me… ye do, do ye not?"

She nodded enthusiastically and the weight of doubt lifted. "Then I shall ne'er take that for granted."

***

When Daimh had said he would never take her for granted, Harper had to wonder if this was his idea of a commitment but hesitated to press him further. But she was worried as to what was on his mind. There had always seemed to be something that held him back. Well, she would hopefully find out soon enough and his words just now were enough to satisfy her… for a while.

137

The tapping on her bedroom door at midnight pleased Harper more than she'd like to admit. To have her mood change so rapidly from apprehension to utter joy was disconcerting. She was quickly falling hard for her warrior—*her* warrior—and was convinced he felt the same. If he would only speak the words, she would certainly feel more secure. But then, he was here, now, and that spoke volumes.

He strode into the room with an expression so serious a chill ran up Harper's spine. At the hearth, he turned, his face an unreadable mask.

"We must talk," he said.

And Harper heard the death knell of their budding romance.

He took her hands and gently pulled her over to the chairs in front of the fire to sit facing one another. Her chest so tight she could barely breathe. Harper strengthened her resolve not to cry. But then, hadn't this been too good to be true?

"I hae a confession," he said quietly. "And some things I need to say." His gaze dropped to the ground, and he inhaled, then looked up at her. "I am falling in love with ye, lass."

Her heart soared, the words so unexpected after his previous announcement regarding a confession. Her smile lifted with her soul. She felt as if she could touch the stars. "And I feel the same, Daimh."

Holding up his hands palms out, she waited for the other shoe to drop. "And…?" she encouraged. Or was that a "but"?

"I hae a secret that I fear will change yer mind. But I cannae go on without sharing it. And you must ne'er repeat it to anyone. Ye must promise."

She anticipated something terrible, but she managed to nod. "I promise."

"I hae a brother."

It took a moment for the words to sink in. A brother? Relief poured through her like a cool breeze on a summer day. A brother? That was his big secret? How could that matter? Angling her head at him, she waited for an explanation.

"He is… he is… a changeling."

Now Harper was completely confused. "I don't understand."

His expression shuttered with apparent disbelief. "Ye do nae ken about changelings?"

"No." She reached for his hands and took them in hers. "Tell me what that means."

He inhaled, expanding his chest, then blew out the breath. "When me brother was born, the fairies took him. In his place, they left Thomas. Me da blamed me mother and he was so ashamed and fearful that he left. Me mother tried for a while, hoping they would return her real child if she was kind to the one they left, but after Thomas was weaned, she gave up all hope and

withered away and died. And I was left to care for the lad."

"That's so awful. I'm sorry. It must have been very hard. How old were you when he was born?"

"Seventeen summers."

"So, you're saying your brother was switched when he was born for a…?"

"Changeling. Aye. That's when the fae, the fairies, take a human child and replace it with one bewitched."

"Why? Why would they do that?" Harper knew about the beliefs in the fairy folk, but she hadn't thought how deeply ingrained these superstitions might be in one so strong and brave as Daimh.

"Because the fairies love to pull pranks and cause mischief for humans. It amuses them."

"And your real brother? What happened to him?"

"I ken not. I keep hoping he will be brought back, but after so long a time, I hae given up hope. I love Thomas. I do. But the clan would ne'er accept him. And if they discovered him, they would see he—disappeared."

"Oh my God."

The idea of a changeling made no logical sense, but this was a time of superstition and mythical explanations for things that otherwise couldn't be explained. Harper deduced that Thomas was not their idea of the way bairns should be and therefore had to have been switched. But the fact that Daimh had cared for the boy regardless of what the others might think expanded her heart and her love for him. Only the kindest of men would take on such a responsibility. "Where is he now?"

"The old woman, Eilidh, cares for him. I dare not let anyone else know, save Ian, since as I said, the clan would not treat him kindly." Sadness clouded his expression. "And he is the most loving of bairns." He ran his hand through his dark hair. "Only Ian knows. And, of course, Eilidh and her daughter Iona. So ye must tell no one. It could have dire consequences for the lad." His subdued words were spoken like a plea.

"You have had him hidden away?"

"Aye. I visit him whenever I can, and I care for both him and the widow with food and clothes and coin." He dropped his shoulders in a gesture of defeat. "So now ye know. I hae no hope you can ever forgive me or consider a future with me."

Harper sprang from her chair and threw her arms around his neck, kissing him soundly on the mouth. "Daimh, oh Daimh, I love you even more now."

He pulled back to look her in the eye, disbelief widening his eyes. "How could ye? I am cursed."

"No. I don't believe that for a moment. You are a wonderful man with a generous heart." Drawing him back to her, she nestled her head against his shoulder. "Can I meet him?"

"Thomas?" Daimh sounded shocked and angry. "I do nae understand. I tell ye my family has been tainted by the fairies and ye wish to see for yerself? Like he was an amusement?" He moved her from his lap and stood to go.

She quickly needed to diffuse his rage. "No. You misunderstand."

She returned to her chair and pressed her palms together as if in a prayer for understanding. "Please hear me out." She pulled him back down into the other chair. With some reluctance borne of years of defensiveness, he sat back down and faced her, his expression wary.

"I love you, Daimh. You are the bravest, kindest, most wonderful man I have ever met. And if you have a brother, a part of your family, of course I would like to meet him. The more I learn about you, the more my love grows. Do you understand?"

She could tell he was internalizing her explanation, but there was still a kernel of doubt reflected in his eyes.

"He is a changeling."

"But you clearly care for him and that is enough for me. I would like the chance to love him, too. If you meant the words spoken, that you love me, how can you deny me including those others you care for in our love?"

He gazed at her as if trying with all his might to see

into her heart. "Ye mean that? It does nae offend ye? Scare ye? Disgust ye?"

A question occurred to her. "How old is your brother?"

"Ten summers."

"He is still a boy. How could I find a boy frightening? If you love him, can't you give me the chance to care for him, too?"

His entire body drooped with relief. "Ye mean it, do you nae? Ye really mean it?"

She slid from her chair and threw her arms around his neck again. Hugging her back with such ferocity she thought her ribs might crack, Harper was joyous.

But suddenly, he guided her back from his body. "But what if we were to wed and have bairns of our own? The fairies might still be angry."

Harper pushed his arms aside and snuggled deeper onto his lap. "Whenever there is a child, there is always a chance that something might go wrong. But that is not a reason not to have bairns."

Daimh gazed at her as if she was the most amazing creature he had ever beheld. He kissed her cheeks, her forehead, her nose, and her lips. The kisses were so passionate, her body caught fire. Desperate for more, she stood, and, taking his hand, led him to the bed.

***

Dawn peeked through the window and illuminated the room with pale wisps of morning. Reaching over, Harper was disappointed that Daimh was no longer in bed with her, but she was comforted that he left again to save her reputation. Sure at this point that their affair was not a secret, she still appreciated the gesture.

She left the bed to wash her face with the icy water in her room's basin. She had changed so much over the past few weeks. Optimistic and relaxed now, she no longer woke up tense, anticipating all the things that needed her involvement. She reveled in the newfound feelings. Some of that was due to the man who made glorious love to her at night. Why, she was even beginning to believe in magic, since what else could all of this be?

Daimh had promised to take her to Eilidh's cottage this afternoon and introduce her to Thomas, his brother and most carefully guarded secret. Did she imagine a boy dressed in all black with a wand and witch hat? Laughing at the image it conjured, Harper was convinced Thomas was born with some imperfection that these superstitious people blamed on his being a changeling. Whatever the problem was, she was determined to love the child as much as Daimh did.

Harper had never thought about having children. She certainly had no proper role models as parents and couldn't imagine how she could possibly succeed in that role. She had heard that once a newborn was placed in its mother's arms, love flowed like a vast river. But was that a myth? Was it possible that could actually happen to her, especially if the father was a man as wonderful and loving as Daimh?

More than anything this morning, she sought the counsel of Skye. Her best friend knew her better than anyone and was always honest.

Chapter Thirteen

Sheer terror ran like a vicious torrent through Daimh's veins. He was on the training field, striking at one man after another in mock battle, honing his skills and theirs and releasing some of the tension that tightened the muscles in his neck. Revealing his deepest secret to Harper was perhaps the most difficult thing he had ever done in his life. Admitting he was madly in love with the lass, he had no choice but to tell her the truth. How could he commit to her and continue to hide his brother? Lying was ne'er a part of a good relationship.

She had said she was fine with it, even anxious to meet Thomas, but how would she feel once she actually saw him? There was no doubt as to his origin. The idea of Harper walking away in disgust was almost more than he could bear.

Ian entered the training field, and none too soon. Daimh knew the laird would offer good advice. Desperate for a rope to hang onto, he approached his friend and indicated they should move to the side of the pitch. Ian, puzzled since he had come to work on his own skills, followed.

"Did ye not wish to challenge me and lose?" Ian teased.

"I need but a moment of yer time."

"Is it advice ye be seeking? About yer love life?" Ian asked, grinning. "Since clearly I am the most knowledgeable." He squared his shoulders in pride.

"I love her."

"Ye must be speaking of Skye's friend, Harper, aye?"

Daimh dropped his gaze. "I hae ne'er felt like this. The lass consumes me every thought. And when she is near…"

Ian smiled "I well know the feeling. 'Tis exactly how I felt when I first laid eyes on Skye." Ian angled his head in question. "Well, Harper did nae take her vows and I understand her husband is dead, so why do ye hesitate?"

Daimh lifted his gaze and sucked in a deep breath. "Thomas. I told her about Thomas. And other than ye, no one else knows. Except the widow and Iona, a course."

Ian leaned forward and pressed his index finger to his chin. "How did she take it?"

"She acted relieved. I hae no idea what she thought I was going to say, but haeing Thomas as my brother did not ruffle her feathers in the least."

"So that's good, nay?"

"I trust her. I just…"

"…hae ne'er been in this place afore. I ken," Ian said. "Does she say she loves ye?"

Daimh nodded. "Aye."

Ian reached over and slapped his friend on the shoulder. "I believe the fairies have tormented ye enough and it is yer time for happiness. I say grab it with both hands."

"And if she is repulsed by Thomas?"

"Daimh, no one could ever be repulsed by him. He is a sweet lad. Did ye ever think the fairies brought him to ye knowing ye would be kind to him and care for him?"

"Yer saying they did this not as a curse?"

"It is possible. So far, has he ever done aught to bring ye harm or trouble?"

"Nay, ne'er."

"Then maybe the fairies meant him as a blessing."

"But me da left and my mother…".

"…might have misunderstood and thought the worst."

Daimh thought about this. "'Tis possible I ken."

"And if yer Harper is not accepting, then ye need to put the desire aside and move on to another. But, I have a strong notion that she would nae be friends with Skye if she was less than you hoped."

If it wasnae so unmanly, Daimh would have hugged the laird.

"Thank ye." Ian had eased his fears and Daimh was filled with relief instead of worry.

Suddenly, the urge to strike at something or someone dissipated and Daimh left the field to gather goods to take to Eilidh and Thomas, ready now to introduce his brother to his love.

***

Harper and Skye approached Neasa, who looked suspicious at their approach.

"Is there something amiss?" Neasa asked.

"Oh, nay. We just had an idea and hoped you would think it a good one."

Neasa lifted a brow and waited.

"I know you saw what happened to Conall," Harper began. "So, we…" she looked over at Skye who nodded encouragement. "…were wondering if you—ye—might be interested in letting me set you up a separate space for healing." Deciding not to wait for a response, she hurried on. "We could take all the sewing instruments and herbs and anything else like that and organize everything in one place so that if there is need, we would be ready."

"Hmmm. We already hae a space in the kitchen," Neasa said.

"True, but this would be out of the way and you would have help. I could use some of what I learned in the future, and it would not be so visible if we needed to use techniques that are new here."

Neasa dropped her gaze and then lifted it, a smile lighting her face. "And if it were not so visible—as ye say—we could do more to help the wounded without being named…".

"…witches." Skye finished the thought.

Neasa's smile grew broader. "It makes sense and maybe I could get some rest." She angled her head. "You know more tricks, do ye?"

Skye and Harper exchanged a look, then turned to Neasa. "We do."

"But we don't wish to take anything that is yours," Harper added.

"Oh, ne'er hesitate aboot that. But I would have one condition. Ye must teach me." She turned to Harper. "What ye did with Conall was amazing."

"We will gladly teach you—ye—all that we know," Harper answered, gaining a nod from Skye.

"There is a space down this way," she said pointing down the corridor. "We could easily move the few things out of it and have the men build us some shelves. Come, I'll show ye." Neasa's enthusiasm was encouraging.

The two followed Neasa into a dingy room down a short hall to the right of the pantry. It wasn't very large, but it could accommodate shelves and a table in the middle. And it was so tucked away, no one would pay any attention once it was set up. Most of the clan would be happy to remove the sick and injured away from where their food was prepared.

"I'll ask some of the men to start today," Neasa said.

"Thank ye," Skye and Harper said together.

"I need to thank ye both. Anything that improves the care and reduces my work is appreciated."

"Well, we'll still need you to help us with all the things you use for cures."

Neasa smiled. "Of course, but, as I said, more knowledge is always welcome."

As Harper and Skye walked away, Harper did a little twirl.

"Ye seem quite pleased. Is it only the makeshift clinic that's lifted your spirits?" Skye asked.

"Can we go for a stroll along the loch?"

The two passed through the main hall and out into the bailey. Greeting people as they went, clan members waved and returned smiles. Harper was filled with a sense of family and peace, something she had never before experienced, and she was loving it. She couldn't wait to share her news about Daimh and his brother and get Skye's take on all of it.

Rumbles portended that the sky was angry and intended to douse them before long. Harper stole a glance upward. It did seem to always be raining or about to. But she was growing accustomed to the weather. And when the mist settled on the land, it was like a soft curtain protecting them from the world.

"Talk to me." Skye must have decided they still had some time before the rain forced them back inside.

"It is a secret, so you cannot repeat this. Although Daimh said Ian knows."

Skye's brow furrowed with concern. "Of course. What is it?"

"Daimh has a brother."

Skye dropped her gaze, pondering this, then looked up again. "I did not know, but I cannot see a problem."

"I think he was born with some kind of challenge. Whether it's physical or mental, I don't know. But Daimh seems to believe his brother is a changeling. Given the age difference, I am thinking he might have Down Syndrome."

"I see. Well, I know you. You know that changeling stuff is just superstitious nonsense, and you don't care about that. You and I both know those children are loving and kind. But I can see how he would wish to keep it a secret from the clan. They don't understand such things and I'm afraid those who are born—different—don't usually survive." She instinctively stroked her belly.

"Your babe will be fine. And I agree wholeheartedly about the secrecy, but Daimh seems to think it might bother me and it's been his reason for holding back on his feelings. I am to meet Thomas this afternoon."

"That is exciting." She reached over and squeezed Harper's arm. "Where is this child?"

"He stays with the widow Eilidh and Iona, which explains why Daimh would have been visiting them and bringing that basket."

"You see. I knew there was a logical explanation."

"I know, but now I'm nervous."

Skye's brow furrowed. "About what?"

"You know, meeting the family. The fifteen hundreds aren't like the twenty-first century. Elaborate courtship didn't kick in until the Regency period. Once I meet his brother, he might want to—you know—get married." Harper couldn't contain her smile at that thought.

Skye grinned back. "And then you can't go back. Win—win."

"You're enjoying this," Harper said, half teasing.

"What's not to like? You get to stay, and you've found a man who will care for you and love you and value you for all that you are. As I said, 'win-win'."

"After Richard, I swore I'd never marry again. And this happened so fast."

"You'd deny yourself happiness because your ex was a horrible, selfish ass? Don't you think that's giving him a little too much control?"

"I suppose you're right. But Skye—my entire life and everything I believed has changed in such a short time. It's almost too much to take in."

"I get that. So take it in like you'd eat an elephant."

Harper scrunched up her face in confusion. "What?"

Skye laughed out loud. "You know, a bite at a time."

"Funny, but I see your point." Harper chewed her lower lip. "Okay, I have no choice but to accept the time travel thing… unless we're both drugged and hallucinating or something." She scanned the countryside with its thick forest, rolling hills, and the citadel Eilean Donan rising from the lochs. "I mean, to quote *The Wizard of Oz,* we're certainly not in Kansas anymore."

"Exactly."

"So there goes that belief—that it wasn't possible."

Skye stood quietly, waiting for Harper to continue.

"Daimh is like no one I've ever met, and I really believe I've fallen in love with the man—which also makes no logical sense since I've only known him for such a short time. The time thing again."

"What you're saying is that the reality does not fit into your preconceived ideas. Which doesn't make it less real. You just have to be more flexible."

Harper laughed out loud. "Flexible? Me? That's like asking you to stop believing in fairy tales."

Skye grinned and nodded. A growl of thunder caught their attention. "So, let's go back before we get drenched, and you can get ready to go with Daimh to meet his brother."

Harper threw her arms around Skye's neck and hugged her hard. "I love you."

"I love you, too."

And together they ran to the castle just as the skies opened and poured rain.

Chapter Fourteen

"Do ye mind getting wet?" Daimh asked as they crossed over to Dornie in an open boat.

Harper laughed. "Isn't it a wee bit late to ask me that?" she teased, wrapping herself in a plaid as the rain cascaded down on them.

"I was a bit impatient now that I've told ye the truth of it. We could hae waited."

"I am anxious to meet your brother. A little rain won't hurt."

He reached across to grab her hand, squeezed, and returned to minding the oars.

Once they touched the shore, he jumped from the craft and tied it to a pole before lifting her out. He stepped back into the boat to retrieve the basket he had brought, then wrapping them both in his larger plaid, he led her up the bank and down a rutted road to the cottage.

The home was set back into the woods barely visible as it squatted back among the trees. The plume of smoke that rose from the crooked chimney promised warmth inside. Foliage offered shelter from the onslaught of the rain as Daimh knocked on the old wooden door.

An older woman swung the door wide and ushered them inside. She was a tiny thing, wrinkled like a prune, but her smile was so kind and welcoming, Harper immediately relaxed. Before Daimh could properly introduce them, a happy cry came from the back and a boy rushed to Daimh, wrapping his arms around the large man's legs.

Daimh hugged him, then gently moved him back.

"Thomas and Eilidh, this is the Lady Harper."

Eilidh wrapped Harper's hands gently in her own and nodded, the gesture comforting .

"Since Daimh ne'er brings visitors here, ye must be someone quite special," Eilidh said gently.

Harper smiled at the comment and then bent down, resting on her heels to greet Thomas. Clearly shy, the child pressed against Daimh.

"Hello, Thomas. I am so happy to meet you. I hope we can be friends." Her sincerity was clear, and Thomas took a step toward her. His grin told her all she needed to know.

Thomas was no changeling. His round face and slanted almond-shaped eyes made his condition clear. He *did* have Down Syndrome. Harper knew she could never explain to Daimh or anyone else here that this was simply a chromosomal issue and definitely not the work of the fairies. Her heart went out to the poor child who was separated from the clan for a condition that made him no less loveable.

Opening her arms, Thomas tentatively stepped into her hug and giggled. "I like ye," he said.

"And I like ye, too," she responded. Standing, she held out her hand for him. "Shall we see what your brother has brought you?"

Nodding enthusiastically, Thomas grabbed for the basket Daimh held and proceeded to dig into it. Eilidh moved next to him and took out the foodstuffs and blankets, leaving a toy that had filtered to the bottom.

153

Screeching in delight, Thomas pulled out a carved wooden horse and hugged it to his chest.

Harper looked at Daimh, her head angled in awe. "Did you carve that?"

"Aye. He loves horses and does nae get much chance to ride."

"We could take him riding," Harper suggested. "I am certain there are places we could go."

Thomas had been distracted by the toy, but when he heard Harper's words, he perked up.

"Ride horse?" he said, hope widening her eyes.

Daimh was skeptical and pulled Harper to the corner and lowered his voice. "What if he's seen? I hae no idea how the clan would treat him. They might even try to hurt him, thinking he's cursed."

"Are there no paths through the woods?"

"Aye, but it is a risk."

"Daimh, I have seen children like Thomas before and the more they are treated like other children, the more they flourish."

Daimh worked his jaw, his tension obvious. "But he is a fairy child. He is not like the other children. Do ye not see that?"

"I see a sweet boy who is full of love." Harper knew she couldn't explain more. It wouldn't make any sense to him, but he was looking at her with such softness in his expression, she wanted to kiss him.

Turning to Eilidh and moving toward her, he spoke quietly. "Any problems?"

"Nay. He is always an easy child. And yer friend is right in saying he is a sweet lad full of love."

They sat for a while, sipping some of the sweet wine Daimh had brought and spoke of pleasantries while

Thomas played with his toy. Harper watched the child and was filled with tenderness.

Thomas moved to Harper and hugged her and she was filled to overflowing with love.

But, too soon, it was time to leave.

"Aye, we must go." He bent down to Thomas. "We must go," he repeated. Tears slipped out of the corners of Thomas's eyes. "No go. Stay."

"I will come again soon. I promise."

"Bring Lady."

Harper stepped up to him and knelt beside Daimh. Thomas angled his body to her, and she wrapped him in a hug. He gave her a quick kiss on the cheek and Harper's heart swelled.

"We will come back soon," she promised, hoping that would be the case. Daimh had hidden the boy to protect him, and Harper knew he would not be so readily accepted by the clan. Poor Daimh had worked so hard for so long to keep Thomas a secret. It broke her heart because it was necessary. But that didn't mean they couldn't visit often and show him affection.

Daimh and Harper thanked Eilidh and took their leave. The walk back to the shore was slow and quiet as they held hands, each lost in thought. As they reached the loch, Daimh turned to her.

"Do ye really not care that Thomas is—different?"

"Thomas is a lovely boy and I think that anyone who is capable of such love and devotion should be valued."

Daimh took a deep breath and reached over to hold her by the shoulders. "Ye could love him?"

"Why would I not?"

"Ye could nae tell anyone. I will nae have him abused."

"I understand. But that doesn't mean we couldn't

155

spend time with him. We could go on outings and rides in the woods, and no one would discover us."

He shook his head. "Ye are the most remarkable of women. And I wish to claim you as me own. Would ye be willing? To be me wife?"

Harper couldn't believe her ears. Was he actually proposing? Looking into the depths of his blue eyes, she saw so much love and acceptance and her heart said yes, yes, yes. But her pragmatic side held her back. If she agreed and they married, what if she decided she needed to return to 2024? But, of course, that was ridiculous. A future in the twenty-first century had nothing to offer. Her real future was here, with this glorious warrior and the lives they would build together.

"More than willing," she answered.

Sweeping her up into his arms, he twirled her around in circles until she was dizzy.

***

As soon as they returned to the castle, Harper sought out Skye. They hastened to an alcove and Harper reached for Skye's hands.

"It went well?"

"It was as I thought. Down Syndrome."

"And?"

"I thought he was adorable. And he hugged me and kissed my cheek." Harper stroked the place Thomas had touched.

"Nice," Skye said, nodding. "But there's more?"

"Daimh asked me to marry him."

Skye's face lit up. "That's wonderful! What did you say?"

Harper could feel the blush in her cheeks. "I said yes, of course."

"Yay! Another wedding. And you're staying! So much wonderful news." Skye clapped her hands. "It's nearly Hogmanay. How would you feel about a wedding on New Year's Eve? You know, starting the new year with a new marriage?"

"It's all so fast. Am I making the right choices, Skye?"

"Daimh is a wonderful man, and he will treat you well. Better than well. He'll do everything in his power to see to your happiness. Can you ask any more than that from a husband? And you love him, too, right? I can tell."

"I do. I guess I'm just not used to…"

"Being happy?" Skye asked.

"Yes."

"Well get used to it. Your life is about to change for the better. So come, we must tell everyone!"

"But you won't mention Thomas? Not even to tell Ian you know."

"Of course not. It's our secret."

***

Hogmanay was only a week away. Not much time to prepare for a wedding, but the women faced the challenge with energy and joy. Freya sorted fabric for the dress and Harper chose a soft wool in the palest blue, which complemented her eyes. Kenna organized the food and Neasa oversaw it all. Neasa had sensed Harper's indecision about remaining and was thrilled that marrying Daimh would assure her continued presence here.

"How can I ever repay you?" she asked Freya as the other woman took measurements.

"Repay me? Ye saved me husband's life. You could ask me for a hundred gowns and it would never come close to making us even."

Happy that her being here had made a positive difference, Harper decided to stop feeling guilty and just enjoy all the preparations. Skye whispered that Daimh had gone to the silversmith and was designing something beautiful for a ring and she assured Harper the cake would be spectacular.

And every night, when the moon rose high and the castle settled into slumber, a tap on her door had her welcoming Daimh into her arms.

"Ye know," she said, grinning, "ye can nae visit the night before. It is bad luck." She had to smile inwardly at her use of Scottish words.

Feigning a pout, he nodded. "Aye. I think I can survive a night or two without ye, but it will nae be easy." Running his knuckles along her jaw sent a shiver of desire into her core. "Speaking of, I must lead a routine patrol tomorrow eve, so I will nae be able to visit. But it will be nice after we are wed to nae longer have to sneak up here in the dark."

"I will be happiest to be able to wake up to ye in the morning."

"Aye. So much to look forward to."

"I am guessing Thomas can nae attend the wedding."

Sadness marred his features, his lips down turning and his eyes clouded.

"Nae unless I can find a way to have him hide in the shadows."

"Oh no, Daimh. That would be terrible. He should ne'er be made to be ashamed like that. It's enough he stays hidden in the cottage, but at least he seems unaware that he cannot be discovered. If you brought him to the castle and forced him to cower in the corners, it could only hurt him. We will visit him afterward and bring him cake."

"Yer heart is so kind. I am the luckiest of men to be able to soon call ye wife."

But Harper's heart ached for the boy, never being able to mingle with the clan. Perhaps she could find a way, but overcoming the ingrained superstition of these people would not be so easy.

Chapter Fifteen

The hour was late when the tap came on her bedroom door. How odd. Daimh was to be away tonight. But, if his plans had changed, she didn't want to miss spending any time with him. Wrapping a bed robe about her, she walked to the door, her heart beating in anticipation.

No sooner was the door opened, Iona sidled her way into the room. Taken aback by the visitor, she closed the door and the other woman leaned back against it.

"I hae no doubt ye are surprised to see me here, but I heard Daimh would be away, and I did nae want to miss me chance to tell ye the truth. Ye deserve it and he hae no right to continue to lie to you." She appeared nervous, her lip twitching and her hands shaking.

The hair on Harper's nape lifted and a shiver crawled up her spine. This couldn't be good, and Harper had a very bad suspicion that no matter what Iona said, Harper wasn't going to like it. This woman had done nothing but glare at her since she arrived and now she wants to impart secrets—to protect her? Iona had to know Daimh had told her about Thomas, so what other secrets could she hope to impart? Harper's gut instinct was to simply throw her out, but curiosity gnawed at her. Deciding to allow Iona to say her peace, she indicated they should sit in the chairs by the fire.

"Nay." She didn't move. "I dare not be caught speaking to you like this or I will suffer."

"Then say what you came to say."

"I ken ye don't like me or trust me."

"Iona, that's simply not true. I have no reason not to like you and I understand you and your mother care for Daimh's brother. That alone is a wonderful thing."

Iona began pacing. "That's why I came to see ye." Stopping suddenly, she pierced Harper with a gaze.

"Is something wrong with Thomas?" Fear scratched at her.

"He is nae... what Daimh told ye."

"I don't understand."

"Thomas is my son."

Confusion swirled. "I still don't understand."

"Mine—and Daimh's."

This made absolutely no sense. Iona had to be making this up. And she had an obvious motive. She wanted Daimh for herself and this lie she was spouting would be a perfect way to get rid of her rival. That is, if Harper had been naïve enough to swallow it.

"I see. But I thought you were a widow."

"Daimh and I concocted this story so no one would suspect we harbored a changeling." She resumed pacing again. "I assume he told ye that Thomas was his brother and he was just kind enough to care for him. But the truth is he is a man unwilling to admit the truth. And his son and I are paying the price."

"What price is that?" Harper was still skeptical, to say the least.

"To nae claim me as his rightful wife."

"I see."

"I hae proof. That's what I came to tell ye. If he

161

promised to marry ye, he cannae. He already has a wife. Me. And a child."

This was one amazing tale. Iona clearly had a huge imagination. Or an ambition to get Daimh to marry her. What she hadn't counted on was that Harper was not so gullible. "Proof? In what form?"

"I took the precaution of haeing the priest write up a parchment that declares our marriage."

Was that possible? "I would like to see that paper."

"O' course you would." Her voice dropped. "I counted on that. But I did nae bring it with me. It is at the cottage. Come with me now and I will show ye."

"I think I'll wait until Daimh returns and talk to him first."

"And see me cast out? If he kens I told ye the truth, he will see to it I am sent away. It would kill my mother, to say naught of the pain it will cause… me son." She shook her head. "Nay. Ye must come now when the castle is asleep so I can prove me story and no one will find out. And then you'll ken the truth of it."

Was it even possible Iona was telling the truth? Could Daimh be so two-faced, so dishonorable, as she claims? Harper had made mistakes in the past. She had thought Richard to be kind and supportive and really, he only wanted her for her money. And once he could lay claim to it as her husband, he showed his true colors.

Would Ian, who seemed like a wise and moral leader, allow this to transpire? For Daimh to be so despicable as to deny his wife and the child he fathered? Would the fact that Thomas was deemed a changeling encourage the laird to keep Daimh's secret?

Harper needed data and the only way to find that was to go with Iona to the cottage. In itself, that was an act of betrayal to Daimh, but then she hadn't known him very long. She needed the truth. And there was that niggling insecurity, planted by neglect from her parents and constant criticism from her ex. There was also curiosity. Harper knew Iona wanted Daimh, but just how far would she go to see her rival disillusioned and willing to take a step back? Yes, she would like to see her *proof.*

"Give me a moment to dress." She grabbed her gown and stockings from the chest in front of the bed. With her back turned, she was careful to tuck the dagger Daimh had given her into a garter, just as a precaution. She was curious, not stupid. She tied the ribbons in the front of the vest and slipped on her shoes.

"Show me," she said to Iona.

Nodding with satisfaction, the woman opened the door and leaned out, checking the corridor. She turned back to Harper. "Ye must be quiet and when we reach the gate, you must tell the guard ye need to tend a sick child. Tell them the child is in a cottage near the landing and ye do nae require escort. They will let you pass."

With the knife pressed firmly against her thigh, Harper did not perceive how this woman could pose any type of physical threat. Unless what she had told Harper was true and then Harper's emotional world would fall apart.

Her heart pounding, Harper followed Iona down the steps, being careful to make as little noise as possible. They slipped out the main door and Iona hurried to the gate with Harper close behind.

"Who goes there?" A guard called down.

"It is I. Harper. I mean the Lady Harper."

Harper glanced to Iona who had pressed herself against the wall, not visible to the man guarding the gate.

"I must tend to a child on the other side of the loch, who has fallen ill. It will nae take me long."

"It is late and ye should nae go by yerself. I will send down an escort," the guard responded.

"No need. "'Tis not far and I shall return quickly."

"Does not sit right to send ye out alone in the dark."

"Please, we waste time while the child suffers."

The guard thought about this for a moment, obviously weighing her words. "If ye hae not returned in an hour's time, I shall send someone for ye. Which cottage?"

She had to think quickly. "The one closest to the loch to the right of the landing."

The gate lifted and Harper slipped through as Iona hugged the wall and eased her way out, still holding the shadows. Once they were away from the castle and headed to the loch, a thought occurred. "Iona, why didn't you show yourself? Surely there would be no harm in my visiting with you and your mother."

Moonlight lit Iona's face and an ugly half smile lifted her lips. It was the smile of victory.

Before Harper could react, a sharp blow smashed into her head and a dark cloth was thrust over her face as the world went black.

***

"Pardon, my lady, but hae you seen the lady Harper this morn?" Daimh's tone communicated his feeling of dread.

He had just returned from a night of scouting and had gone directly to Harper's room. Being away from her was a new torture he had never experienced before, and he sought to soothe the ache. When he had hastened to her chamber and found her bed undisturbed, a bad feeling in his bones told him that something was amiss.

"She is not in her chamber?" Skye asked.

"Nay. And I have sought her in the kitchens and the hall. No one has seen her this morning."

"Well, she wouldn't just disappear."

A look of panic crossed her face. Skye suddenly turned and ran up the stone steps to Harper's room. He caught up to her as she dropped to her knees beside the bed, and pulled out Harper's bag, and rummaged through it. She grabbed hold of something inside and sat back on her heels, breathing a sigh of relief.

"My lady?" Daimh asked. Now he was completely baffled. What did whatever was in that bag have to do with Harper not being in the castle?

Skye hesitated, then pressed her lips together. "She would not leave without this," she said, indicating the carrier.

"Do ye ken where she might have gone. 'Tis still early."

Skye was quiet for a few moments, clearly thinking. "I don't ken. But this is nae like her." A thought seemed to strike. "Would she hae gone to visit... someone in Dornie?"

"Ye ken, do ye not?" The edge of betrayal was blunted by the fact that, although it was clear Harper had told her about Thomas, there was no judgment in her question.

"Daimh, she only told me because she was so happy ye had shared yer secret. She confessed her love and was worried that before ye told her about yer brother ye were holding back. And when you confessed about him, she loved ye so much more."

165

Hearing this from another, especially from the lips of Harper's closest friend, warmed his heart. Knowing about Thomas increased her love for him. It was a small miracle.

"To answer yer question—I can go and see."

"In the meantime, I shall ask everyone to help look for her."

Fear clenched in his gut as he rowed to Dornie and hurried to Eilidh's house. He was a knot of anxiety. His mind whirred with all sorts of horrible ideas of what may have befallen Harper. And he felt the need to check on his brother. Whoever took Harper may have also come here. By the time he reached the cottage, he was overly distraught. He pounded on the door until Eilidh swung open the portal, her brow was creased with worry.

"Daimh?"

"Is the lady Harper here? Is Thomas well?"

She seemed confused. "Is there a problem?"

Just then, Thomas threw himself into Daimh's legs and hugged him. "I miss you when yer not here," the boy whined.

"I ken, lad. I promise to return soon, but now I must find the lady Harper. Ye hae not seen her hae you?"

The boy shook his head. "Maybe Iona knows. But I do nae think she slept here last night."

Turning to Eilidh, his eyes widened. "Is that true?" Nothing made sense now. Was Iona in danger, as well. Or was Iona's jealousy the reason Harper was nowhere to be found. Was that possible? Daimh knew she wanted him, but to harm another to further her cause? It was unthinkable.

Eilidh frowned and hurried back into the cottage to check the cot where Iona usually slept. "Thomas is right.

Her bed is still made. But I didnae hear her leave, so it must hae been after I went to bed. Or it's possible she slipped out early this morn."

Daimh bent down to Thomas. "I will come back soon, I promise."

"Maybe Iona found a man friend," Eilidh suggested, her tone hopeful. But Daimh was already up and running to the loch, fear clutching at his insides.

Chapter Sixteen

She had been thrust into a wagon and carted over rutted roads for days. A man with as rough a face as his disposition stood guard, glaring at her, and sneering when she tried to speak. He reeked of sweat and onions and the smell made her nauseous. Someone had thrust a filthy blanket over her to help keep the cold at bay, but it too smelled like it had been well used by animals before it ended up here.

When they stopped along the way, an old man would step into the wagon and offer her water and stale bread, which she gratefully accepted. The old man refused to answer any of her whispered questions, merely bidding her to be quiet or suffer the consequences. Her throbbing head encouraged her to listen to his warning. Her head ached and dizziness came and went, leading her to believe she had a concussion. Forcing herself to stay awake or sleep only in short spurts was not too difficult, since the bouncing of the wagon was relentless.

Her hands had been bound in front of her and her ankles were tied together. A blindfold was tied around her head, blocking her vision. Her head still felt like it had been stuffed with cotton and now everything was dark. And terrifying.

Two men lifted her and carried her through a heavy

door, then flung her down on a hard stone floor, her body twisted into a pretzel. Her energy sapped, she did not even try to resist.

"Yer certain she's a Forbes." The man who spoke had a voice that was unfamiliar to her ears.

"Aye. And she has set her sights on Daimh MacRae."

But this voice. This one she distinctly recognized. *Iona.*

"It will tear him apart to have her gone," the conniving girl said. "Ye should be able to get her weight in gold when you ask for a ransom. And get your revenge at the same time."

Harper should never have underestimated Iona's jealousy. She could only wonder where they had taken her. Knowing she had been unconscious from the moment she was out of sight of the castle gates and not able to tell if it was night or day, and being so unfamiliar with the area itself, Harper had no idea how far away she had been taken from Eilean Donan. She was only aware it had been days, which meant they could be anywhere.

So, they planned to hold her for ransom. But it was also for revenge, and she had no idea what that meant. She had watched enough crime TV to know that usually didn't go very well for the kidnapped victim. But then, this was the sixteenth century and maybe there might be a different outcome. She could only hope.

Until the man spoke again.

"Or I may just send her back in pieces. It would serve them right for Corrichie. But the goal is to release Adam."

Her blood chilled and panic nearly stopped her heart at their words.

"Or maybe do both? Secure Adam's release and

then send her back in pieces." Iona again, laughing this time.

She was to be a means to get back a prisoner taken at Corrichie. If Harper ever found her way out of this, Iona would regret this betrayal. That vow kept Harper's spirits up, even as she was lifted and taken down a flight of steps. Dropped onto another stone floor, she managed to roll, stopping only when she struck a hard wall. The sound of a creaking door and the finality of it snapping into place resonated in her bones. And the smell. Death and decay and wet earth. It was the dungeon, but whose and where?

By dragging her head across her shoulder, she managed to dislodge the cloth over her eyes enough to gauge her surroundings. It was a dungeon alright. The walls dripped with fetid moisture and the darkness was broken only by the tiniest sliver of light from a high slit of a window and some torches burning along the far wall. The mud floor oozed with only God knew what. And outside the bars, she could make out a rotting pile of wood off to the right. This was a place prisoners went to rot away and die.

She had been so stupid to trust Iona. No one saw her go except the guards and she had given them a plausible excuse. And thinking back, they hadn't seen Iona at all. There was no way anyone would know where she was.

She was so cold. And wet. The skittering of creatures made it clear the rats were making plans for her. Scooting back into a corner, she brought her knees to her chest to stop the shivering.

A thought flitted briefly. Would Skye and Daimh think she had just up and left? No! Skye would check for the cloak and when she found it, she would know Harper was still in the sixteenth century. And she would reassure

Daimh. But what good would it do? They would have no idea where to begin to look for her and she was terrified she would die here. And in a hideous way after being tortured. Cut up into pieces. Now she was shivering from fear as well as the freezing temperature.

No! She would not give up. A mantra she remembered screamed in her head: Everything will be okay in the end and if it's not okay, it's not the end. It's not the end! It's not the end!

They had mentioned revenge for Corrichie. Harper took a deep breath and tried to remember what Skye had told her about that. It was a battle. And the clans, including the MacKenzies and MacRaes, banded together to fight for Queen Mary under William 7th Lord of Forbes. It happened near Aberdeen. The clans had battled the Gordons and afterward, one of the Gordons had died suddenly, perhaps from heart failure, and another had been executed after the resounding defeat. But one more had been captured. That was no doubt the Adam they spoke of. No wonder her captor wanted to assure himself she was a Forbes. And to add insult to injury, after the battle, Lord Forbes would have been awarded Gordon lands by the Queen which would have further infuriated the losing Gordons. So if they could get their kinsman back and punish the Forbes in the process…

A sickening acknowledgement of this history made it clear to Harper she was doomed.

It was so unfair. She had finally accepted time travel as a reality and found true love in Daimh after a lifetime of dreaming of a decent man to love her, only to have it snatched away so cruelly. The best she could hope for was a quick death.

***

Daimh was losing his mind. He had searched every inch of the castle and grounds. He verbally abused the guards who did not stop her from leaving the night before, but instead opened the gate for her. He restrained himself from beating the careless men to death. Did they not think something was amiss? The fools! Conall and Errol, Ian's brother-in-law, had gone to Dornie and knocked on every door, but no one had seen her last night. So where had she gone? And why?

And where was Iona? Instinct gnawed at him, reminding him again that she desired him. Could her jealousy have led her to harm Harper?

The members of the clan gathered in the great hall, frustration evident in their expressions. Lady Skye's eyes were red from crying and Ian was trying to comfort as well as lead a more thorough search.

Ian directed himself to Daimh. "Ye said she told the guards she had to tend a sick child."

"Aye," he responded, "and nay there no sick bairn in the village. Conall and Errol questioned everyone. No one sent for her for any reason. It was a lie to get her to leave the confines of the castle."

Errol spoke up then. "We found fresh cart tracks on the other side of the loch leading west. And there was evidence of at least two men walking just out of sight of the castle walls."

"If they meant to take Harper, they would have had to carry her. She would not go with strange men without protest, would she?" Daimh looked to Skye for confirmation.

"Nay. Knowing her, she would have fought like a

demon. Unless…" Skye's voice broke as she sobbed with the realization Harper had to have been knocked out.

"She is a strong lass. She will be fine." Ian said, comforting his wife. "Is anyone else missing?" he demanded.

"Iona," Daimh spat, his eyes narrowing with fury. "If that lass has done aught to hurt Harper…"

"Could she have been taken, too?" Conall asked.

Daimh forced himself to inhale to exact some calm. "I think it was she that arranged this."

"That is a rough accusation," Errol responded.

"Aye, but the facts support it," Daimh answered. "Harper was the only one seen leaving, which means she was lured out of the grounds somehow. It would be possible for someone to cling to the walls and slip out behind her without being seen. Two sets of small footprints led away from the castle, one set verra close to the wall. Then, only one set joined with those of the men. Why would another conceal themselves unless there was some evil motive?" Daimh dragged his fingers through his hair in anger.

"And it is Iona that is missing, ye said?" This from Ian.

"Aye. Her mother said she has been gone since last night. Or mayhap verra early this morn."

"But why would Iona do such a thing?" Conall asked.

Skye stepped up then. "Seriously? Were the actions of Davina so distant that ye cannot remember what jealousy will do to an unscrupulous woman? Iona has had her cap set for Daimh for as long as I've been here. But when he preferred Harper…" She let the last words speak for themselves.

"But who and why would anyone help her?" Conall asked.

"Did the Gordons not just suffer at the hands of the Forbes, as well as the other clans. And is Harper not a Forbes?" Ian asked.

"Gordon lands are in Aberdeenshire," Errol stated. "And Adam Gordon is still being held captive."

"Then we must plan another assault on the damnable Gordons. And I hae no doubt the Forbes will join us to save one of their own." Daimh was feeling more positive. He was a man of action and putting a plan in motion helped quell some of his rage into positive energy.

"Aye," Ian responded, "but we must wait for affirmation it is the Gordons who have her."

"Who else would it be?" Daimh demanded.

"We do not know for certain, but I am convinced whoever is responsible will show their hand soon enough."

***

Meager light from the torches cast deep shadows upon the bleak stone walls, punctuating how alone and lost she was. Panic gave way to forced calm, which would retreat again into brutal terror.

Harper guessed she had been in this hellhole for two days. No one had entered her cell , not to release her bindings, nor to bring food or water or to empty the chamber pot. Her arms and legs had gone numb from the bindings, her mouth as dry as if filled with desert sand and her ribs ached. Her breathing was not impeded, and so she hoped no bones had been broken. At least she was able to see once she managed to remove the cloth from her face and her eyes had adjusted. But the damp, miserable cold was so permeating she could not stop the shivering.

Remembering the threes of survival—three minutes without air, three days without water, three weeks without food—did not help her state of mind. Her time was running out. Chances are they did not wish her to die from dehydration. And that faith kept her gaze on the bars of her cage, praying for someone to bring her water. Hypothermia might end her before she could be rescued, but she had heard it was not an unpleasant way to die. But then, was there a pleasant way?

With too much time to think, she went through the stages of grief: anger, denial, bargaining with God, sadness, depression. Refusing to progress to acceptance, she intended to hold on as long as possible. Maybe, by some miracle, Daimh and Skye would figure out that Iona had betrayed her, and they would determine where she had been kidnapped. After all, this entire journey was fanciful, so she may as well pretend it would be okay, right?

This was all her fault. If she hadn't been so insecure, so gullible, she never would have followed Iona. Here she was, Harper the pragmatist, who failed to use logic before giving in to her feelings of inadequacy. Beating herself up now was useless. She had to concentrate on using any advantage to get out of this mess. She was not a helpless female. She had hundreds of years of knowledge and a brain. If she remembered who she was, she might just be able to figure something out.

One thing was unfortunately becoming more and more certain. She was going to die here, alone, cold, hungry. And she knew Skye would bear the guilt. That thought made her sadder than anything. None of this was Skye's fault. Harper's best friend had found a painting at an estate sale and decided it was possible to travel through time to find the subject of her obsession. She had been right. That Harper chose to follow her was Harper's choice. And ending up here? Well, Harper had no one to blame but herself.

And Daimh. Such a wonderful man. Her heart ached for his suffering, knowing he loved her and would miss her as much as she now missed him. And he, too, would lay blame at his own feet for failing her. If only cell phones existed, she could text them, let them know they weren't to blame. Ah, but the irony would be no service in this pit.

Footsteps in the corridor sent her pulse into overdrive. Were they coming to kill her now? Before the thought could coalesce into pure terror, a small figure appeared at the bars. The girl looked to be in her late teens, all angles and bones. Her hair hung to her waist, a lifeless tangle of what might have been red or blonde, but it was hard to tell in the dim light. Her left eye was swollen nearly shut and she limped as she walked. And a ragged scar stretched from the corner of her right eye to her chin. In her hands, she carried a bowl and a set of keys hung from a belt around her tiny waist, tugging at the fabric of a dress two sizes too large.

"I am Fenella. I am to be yer keeper. I hae water and if I open the door and ye try to push past me, the guard at the top of the steps will end your life. There is no escape. And if ye happen to get away from me, even though the man will stop ye, they will kill me as well. Do ye ken?"

Harper nodded. If this slip of a girl would continue to visit, there would be a better opportunity to get away, especially if she gained her trust. Harper had to find out more about the place where she was being held. Maybe even discover a secret passage or an escape route. Today they would be expecting her to try to run, but hopefully after a little time, they would relax the guard and she would have a much better chance at leaving here alive. Especially if this girl could help.

"I will stay at the back of the cell," Harper said. It was not easy to maneuver with her hands and feet tied, but she managed to inch her way further backward on her bottom.

Moving slowly and nearly tipping over twice, she made it to the far wall, then watched as the girl fumbled with the keys and finally opened the door. It creaked in protest but swung wide enough to let her inside. She placed the bowl on the ground and quickly backed out, closed the entry, and clicked the lock into place.

"Will you stay with me for a bit?" Harper asked.

"Nay. But I will bring ye bread this night." And she scurried away.

Harper scooted over to the bowl and was thrilled to see it filled with clear water. Lifting the vessel carefully with both hands, she was able to bring it to her mouth. Pacing herself so she did not drink too quickly and throw it up. She swallowed gratefully even as it left odd aftertaste on her tongue. Darkness edged her vision as she realized her mistake and, unable to fight whatever they had put into the water, she sank back to the floor.

Chapter Seventeen

"I say we go now," Daimh demanded, then resumed the pacing he seemed unable to control. The days of inaction, worry and fear for Harper had been the darkest of his life.

Just then Errol came running into the great room with a parchment held out in front of him. "This just arrived by messenger," he panted, having run from the gate.

Ian grabbed the missive and opened it as a piece of short blonde hair fell to the stone floor.

"Is that Harper's hair?" Daimh didn't want it to be true.

Quickly reading the message, Ian raised his head. "It is from the Gordons. They have her and sent the hair as proof."

Daimh scooped up the hair and rubbed it between his fingers and nodded. "Aye, it is hers." His voice caught and he swallowed hard, sick with the thought of her being taken captive. "What else does it say?"

"They demand an exchange. They ask that we petition the Forbes to release Adam Gordon in trade for the lady. But they assure us that Harper is still alive."

He had to think clearly and without the emotion that was choking him. He shook his head. "Nay. I do not trust them. I say we gather our forces and get Lady Harper back. And may the devil take those who have done her harm."

Ian stepped up behind him and put a calming hand on his shoulder. "We will send word to the Forbes to join us. Ye need nae worry. They hate the Gordons and will nae doubt be eager to help. And the greater our show of force, the more likely the Gordons are to give up." Ian turned to the men. "Prepare to ride."

Rory, one of the grooms, stepped forward. "I wish to accompany you, Laird."

"Thank ye, lad, but ye are a groom, not a fighter."

"I hae been practicing with a claymore. Errol can attest to it."

Ian looked over to his brother-in-law, who nodded.

"I ken ye know I betrayed the Lady Skye because I was lied to by a wicked woman, and yet yer lady saved me life when I had the plague. 'Tis the least I can do to help redeem meself and save her friend."

Ian nodded his approval and the boy scurried away while Ian opened his arms to bid goodbye to Skye.

"I'm going with ye," Skye said.

"Nay, my love. Ye have our child to think of. And if I must worry about yer safety, I will nae be able to concentrate on the task at hand."

"Bring her back," she said, tears tracing yet another trail down her cheeks.

"I will. Ye have me word."

Following directly behind Ian, Daimh pulsed with fury and bloodlust. "I will kill them all," he vowed.

***

Blinking awake, Harper was stiff and sore, but not quite as cold. Her head throbbed, no doubt from being drugged. As she slowly sat up in effort not to make the pain worse,

179

she realized the bindings around her hands and feet were gone. And a filthy plaid blanket had been draped over her. Small blessings. She supposed she was not to die just yet.

Soft footfalls in the corridor alerted her that Fenella was returning. The girl appeared outside the bars, this time with a hunk of bread and another bowl of water. Without a word, she opened the door, the hinges groaning, and slipped into the cell.

Harper glared at her with narrowed eyes. "I want no more of your tainted water," she spat at the girl.

Fenella dropped her gaze. "I had nae choice. But I promise this water is clean."

Raising her eyebrows in doubt, Harper watched as Fenella took a sip of the water, then held out the bowl. Greedily, Harper accepted it and swallowed gulps of the cold liquid. The girl then offered the bread, which Harper eyed with suspicion.

"It, too, is safe," Fenella assured her.

Harper took the bread and bit into it. It was stale and tasteless, but it was food. "Then why was I poisoned?" she asked between bites.

"They wanted to cut off yer hair to send with their demands. I told them ye would not fight, but the men have their own ways. And when they left, I cut yer bindings. There was no need for them."

Harper instinctively touched her hair and felt the missing shank on the side. "Thank you for releasing me from the bindings."

"I am hoping ye will nae hurt me now that ye are unbound."

"No, I won't. I promise."

"But when the men return, ye must use the ropes to look as if ye are still tied. Otherwise, I will suffer the punishment." She hesitated. "'Tis not that I hae loyalty to ye. I just hae none to them."

"Again, I promise. I am grateful for your kindness."

"I do nae envy ye. The clan is not forgiving and knowing ye are Forbes raises their ire."

"And what of the woman who arranged all this and saw to my being here?"

"She is gone. I ken she sensed they planned to do away with her, since she was nae longer any use to them, so she fled. They did nae give chase since she has nowhere to go." The girl gave a chocked laugh. "She made a point to find her way here and tell them of ye, a hated Forbes, no doubt hoping for a reward. But, men that they be, they played her for a fool." Fenella shrugged. "She'll nae doubt die before she makes it back to yer clan." She shrugged again.

"You do not pity her?" Harper asked.

"She betrayed another out of spite. It isnae right what she did to ye. I suppose I am doing the same. Betraying the clan, I mean. But ye are nae guilty of anything except being born a Forbes."

So this woman had a sense of honor. That was always a plus.

Harper thought before to ask why she was enslaved, but Fenella had just answered the question. She was a pawn in a clan game and knowing more would not help her now. No, now she needed to befriend this girl-woman and find out what she could about a possible escape.

Knowing Daimh and Skye would probably move heaven and earth to find her did not mean they would reach her in time. Her captors may grow tired or angrier and just execute her because they could. She could not wait for anyone to rescue her. She had to try to find her way out of this herself.

"Who are you?" Harper asked.

The girl cocked her head, as if it was a question she had never before pondered.

"I suppose I am the wife of Alex Gordon."

Harper didn't bother to try and explain the girl was a person in her own right. "But you are so young."

The girl straightened her spine. "I am sixteen summers."

"And the wounds? The bruises?"

"I deserved them all. I am an imperfect wife." Tears coursed down her cheeks and Harper longed to comfort the girl, but any such move might be interpreted negatively.

"I do not believe it. I think you are very kind-hearted."

"That is not a good thing," Fenella whimpered. "I am weak and stupid."

"No. You are not. You mustn't believe that. And you do not deserve to be hurt." Harper shook her head. "How long?"

"Hae I been marrit? Two years, three months, eight days."

Poor child. Married off so young and more than two years in living hell.

The girl spun on her heels and nearly ran out the door, locking it behind her. She sniffed once, lifted her chin, and was gone.

***

It should have taken three days to ride to the Forbes castle, but Ian and Daimh and the others totaling one hundred made it in two and a half. Making certain their horses

182

were cared for, they were ushered into the main hall where they were received by Lord Forbes and offered food and drink, which the men gratefully accepted.

"Your message said the bastard Gordon hae taken one of mine?" Lord Forbes asked, his jaw tight.

"Aye," Ian answered. "The lass grew up in France with me wife and is to wed me man Daimh."

Daimh stepped forward, nostrils flaring. "They wish to trade for your captive Adam Gordon."

"I see. Well, then the Gordons hae brought more bloodshed on themselves. They do not learn that they cannot win, and this will only increase the ire of the Queen as well. Their holdings are not far, although what is theirs shall soon be mine, forfeit to me from Mary. They will rue the day they failed to accept their losses."

"When can we ride?" Daimh tried to contain his impatience and was failing.

"At sunrise. I can spare two hundred to ride with ye and, along with yours, that should be enough to see to the release of the lass. And teach the Gordons yet another lesson."

Ian nodded his thanks.

"In the meantime, rest, eat and drink. Have no fear, the Gordons will regret their impunity."

***

Harper heard the celebrations of the certain return of Adam Gordon, the men above convinced she was the bargaining chip they required. But Harper, ever the realist, was certain this was too easy. It didn't make sense that a simple prisoner exchange was all that was happening.

For one thing, she was a female and in this day and age, women had little value. The Gordons had to be using her as a more than just a token. Their game was revenge for Corrichie. They were hoping to lure the MacKenzies and the Forbes into a trap. But the nature of that trap was impossible to guess. Logic dictated something very bad was planned, but she had no idea what that could be.

Her faith had to rest in Ian's battle acumen. He was no fool, nor was Daimh. But she worried Daimh might let his heart rule over his common sense and put himself in harm's way. If anything were to happen to him—she could not even begin to entertain that thought.

Her only hope to aid them was to glean information from Fenella and try to find a way to let the clan know what the trap was to be. Knowing there was an ambush would only help so far. If she could let them know the details, that would definitely be helpful. Ah, but she was a fool. She was stuck in this pit with no means of escape. Frustration preyed upon her. She desperately wanted to do something.

Suddenly, she remembered the knife in her garter. How could she have forgotten? Must have been the dehydration and exhaustion. She ran her hand along the leather sheaf and found the weapon inside reassuring. She was not totally defenseless. But a knife against more than one or two men would prove ineffectual. Still, it was comforting to know it was there.

A tapping of footsteps had her moving to the bars. Fenella was sneaking down the corridor, looking behind her as if to assure herself she was alone. When she reached the cell, she pressed her index finger to her lips to indicate Harper should be quiet.

Unlocking the door and opening it very slowly so it

184

would not make noise, she slipped inside and closed the entry behind her. Gently, she pushed Harper to the back of the space. It was then, as a ray of light from one of the torches on the wall washed across Fenella's face, that Harper saw her cheek was swollen and bloody.

"Me husband is angry with me."

Harper shook her head. "Is it because of me?" She sincerely hoped not. This poor child had suffered so much already, Harper didn't want to be responsible for more.

"Nay. I hae not given him an heir and me courses hae returned. He said I have no worth, and when he is no longer preoccupied with ye, he will set me aside."

"Is that a bad thing? To be set aside from him? He beats you."

"But where will I go? I have nowhere to go." Sobs racked her frail body.

"I think if you ate more, you might have a better chance at having a child—a bairn."

Fenella tilted her head in obvious confusion. "That makes nae sense."

"If a woman does not have enough meat on her bones, she cannot grow a child. It is true."

"Then I am lost, for Alex says I eat too much as it is."

"Lovely man," Harper sneered. "But I have an idea."

"Aye?"

"Help me escape and come with me. I am certain the MacKenzies will take you in and you will have a better life. Those men treat their wives with love and respect."

"Ye jest with me."

"No. My best friend is married to the laird, and he is very good to her."

"Ye are not even from the Highlands. Yer speech is strange and ye are nae like the other wummen I know."

185

"I was raised in France," Harper answered, hoping this was enough of an explanation.

"I nae if it is even possible. There is a way out of here, but if we're caught, it is certain death. I cannae help ye. I am too frightened."

"I understand. But perhaps you could tell me the way out."

Boots pounding down the steps and along the corridor silenced them. Fenella pushed Harper further back and, grabbing the ropes, threw them to her. Heart pounding, Harper pressed herself into the far wall and wrapped the bindings around her wrists and ankles.

"What do ye here?" the man demanded, holding a torch high. "Ye are but a worthless waste, so ye best have a good explanation."

Cowering against the side wall, Fenella's breath came in quick pants of fear. "Ye said I should check on her."

The man glanced over at Harper, squinting in the meager light. Taking a step closer to her, he eyed Harper with interest.

"For a Forbes, ye are comely."

Harper could read his thoughts and they sent a shiver up her spine.

"I may need to avail meself of yer charms before yer... release." His smirk did not ease Harper's fears. "That baggage..." he angled his head to Fenella, "...I have no need of her meager body. But ye..."

Leaning down and reaching out, he grabbed her left breast and squeezed. Harper's bile rose and she wished she could vomit on him, but she had eaten too little in the last days. She might have swung at him, but she promised Fenella she would fake being still bound.

186

"Aye, there is a handful," he chortled. Before he could do anything else, a man's voice echoed down the corridor. "Alex, Clan Seton's men are arriving."

Alex huffed a regret, then spun on his heel to face Fenella. "Bring a bucket and bathe her. She smells like a pig's arse." Turning back to Harper, he leered at her. "Reinforcements to see our plan succeeds. Maybe I shall give ye to Adam as a welcome home present once I have done with ye." He faced Fenella again. "Get her washed. And then get to the kitchens and see to the food and drink for our guests." And he was gone.

Harper breathed a sigh of relief. She peered over at Fenella, who was also breathing easier. It was only a temporary reprieve from what Alex had planned for Harper's future, but it was something.

***

Following her husband's instruction lest he become violent toward her again, Fenella left and returned with a bucket of water and some cloths for washing.

"It cannae hurt to wash off some of the filth of this place." Fenella said. Though she offered a tiny smile, her drooping shoulders implied Harper's outcome was grim.

There were no worries for them about her rescue now. The Gordon clan was being joined by another and they were feeling strong.

"Clan Seton's men?" Harper asked as she wiped a wet rag over her face.

"Aye. From what I heard, Seton will send enough men to protect the castle and ensure they gain the release of Adam. Then, they intend to fight, since Clan MacKenzie is now their sworn enemy. They are sure that

Clan MacKenzie cannot gain reinforcements so quickly and Alex is counting on their delay."

"Why would Clan Seton offer aid?" Harper asked.

"They have long since pledged their allegiance to Clan Gordon. It is the way of things. Clans join together and stay loyal to one another until it changes." Fenella lifted her hands in a shrug, the whole alliance thing an obvious mystery.

"Then my only hope is escape."

"Then ye have no hope at all. Ye are a Forbes, sworn enemy to both Gordons and Setons."

"But if we work together..." Harper knew it was futile, but she had no other choice than to try to gain this girl's cooperation, which may or may not be of use.

"Lady, I am only a woman. I hae no power. I would aid you if I could, but I, too, am helpless and a prisoner here. I am only here to bear my husband's frustrations."

"No. You mustn't think like that. You are a kind girl. A girl with honor. And I believe you can be strong. If I can find a way away from this place, I give you my pledge that I will take you with me and find a better life."

Fenella gave her a wan smile. "I wish I could believe that to be possible."

Chapter Eighteen

Ian and Daimh led the group of hundreds as it approached the Gordon castle. More a manor house than a stronghold, it was surrounded by woods and situated not on a hill but instead on flat ground. Choosing to stay back out of sight in the trees until they agreed on the best approach, the leaders gathered in a makeshift tent furnished with a small table and several chairs.

John, Master of Forbes, stepped forward.

"I hae never been inside, but I hae no doubt there is a dungeon. And that is certainly where they would be keeping the lady. It would be too easy for her to escape otherwise, and they would lose their advantage."

"Then we shall surround the place and kill them all," Daimh said, his voice low and menacing.

"They will be expecting an attack and will probably bring Harper out to stop us from a siege. Instead, what if we suggest a negotiation?" This from Ian.

"You would bargain with these animals for Harper's life?" Daimh's outrage puffed his cheeks. "Would that be your idea if it was the Lady Skye?"

Ian patted Daimh on the shoulder. "Listen to me. I do nae think they are expecting a force of hundreds. If we can act as if we are but a few come to talk, we can ask that they prove she is still alive. We will demand to be taken to her and once a few of us are there to protect her, the others can attack."

"Aye," agreed John. "Any other way might put her life in danger."

The unspoken was that she might be dead already and that was one thought Daimh dismissed at once. He had waited his whole life for a woman like Harper and he would never accept she could be taken from him. It would mean the end of him.

***

The pounding of boots on the steps caught their attention. Fenella pressed herself against the side wall outside the cell, seeming to vanish into the shadows. Reassured she was not alone, but terrified by what whoever was coming had in store, Harper took a deep breath and curled into a ball against the back of the cell, remembering again to wrap the ropes about her wrists and ankles.

Alex Gordon swung the door wide. "*Gorach galla*," he spat, obviously referring to Fenella. "Cannae even be trusted to lock the gate." He approached Harper like a stalker reveling in the sight of his prey. Her heart lurching and beat uncomfortably against her ribs, she tried to affect calm. She was certain he would thrive on her fear, and she refused to give him the satisfaction.

Hovering above her, he grinned, his eyes reptilian. "Did ye think to be rescued?"

Harper pressed her lips together, refusing to play his game. If this was to be her fate, she would embrace it. Well, maybe not embrace, but certainly not act the coward.

"*A bheil iad a' smaoineachadh* as if I do nay ken they hide in the woods?"

Even though Harper did not understand Gaelic, she got the gist of what he was saying. Her clan—yes, her clan—meaning Daimh and the others, had come to rescue her. A thrill of hope wiggled through her, and she had to work to suppress the pleasure she felt. *Keep your expression neutral,* she counseled herself. *Give him no indication the news affects me.* But she was worried the pounding of her heart was discernible in the quiet of the cell.

The man knew her clan had come to get her. They'd lost the element of surprise. But she had to have faith. They had won at Corrichie, and they would be victorious here. But the reality was Harper was trapped in a cell with an animal. When they came to save her, would it be too late?

Grabbing her by the ankles, he pulled her onto her back away from the wall. The action caused the ropes to fall away. Digging his nails into the flesh of her legs, he shook his head. "*Gorach galla.* Did she think untying you would end well? For either of you? Me wife, she is a waste of air and food. But when I have finished with ye, I will see to her. For now…" He grinned again, with the look of one who enjoys inflicting pain. "And nae ropes makes it so much easier to spread yer legs."

Rape? He intended to rape her now? Was he mad? His castle was under siege, and he was thinking of lust? Well, the knife attached to her garter was going to dissuade him of that notion.

"And once I hae had me way, I intend to throw you to those dogs in bits and pieces."

Neutral, keep your expression neutral, she reminded herself again, although cold terror was seeping into her bones. *Wait for the right moment or he will wrest the dagger away. Patience.*

191

Shifting his plaid so the skirt was thrown over his shoulder, his manhood stretched forward in anticipation. He dropped to his knees, grabbed her wrists, and pinned her arms above her head. The move was quick, too quick. He jammed his knee between her thighs and thrust them apart. "Ye may nae enjoy this, but I certainly will," he promised.

Her hands pinned, she knew she couldn't reach the weapon before he had violated her and her ribcage tightened, pressing on her. She writhed and tried to kick him off, but he was too large, too strong. His twisted smirk made it clear he was enjoying her fight. But the moment of action had come and gone. And if he discovered her blade, he would certainly use it on her. Oh, God. This couldn't be happening. One thought. She had one thought. *I'm so sorry Daimh. I love you.*

In that brief moment, a flash of movement behind him caught her eye. Fenella, her years of misery at his hands played out in her expression, as she lifted a thick piece of wood she had grabbed from the pile near the cell. Leaning back, she swung it, connecting with his head in a satisfying crunch. But she was small and weak and only managed to knock him aside. But before he could react, she swung again. And again. And once more.

Alex was thrown off Harper by the force of the blows. Immediately, she scrambled away from him. He lay limp beside her.

Harper's mouth dropped open in shock and relief. Respect for the mouse of a girl who had finally found her power brought a smile to her face. "Impressive," Harper said. "Thank you."

"Is he… is he dead?" Fenella choked.

Blood dripped out from the back of his skull, and it

appeared he wasn't breathing. She crawled on hands and feet close enough to feel for a pulse at his throat. Harper confirmed he no longer lived. She shook her head in answer to Fenella's question.

Fenella crumpled to the floor.

"You saved me." Harper crouched beside Fenella. "But now we have to leave before anyone finds out."

The girl didn't move except for the heaving of her breath and the sobs racking her. Harper shook her by the shoulders. "Fenella, we must go. And now."

Commotion from above seemed to finally reach Fenella and she stood, shaking off the tears. "I know a way out. The men will be too busy organizing for the attack to pay much attention, but that will only be for a few minutes before they seek Alex for instructions. Come."

Leaning out and checking the corridor, Fenella led the way down a dark corridor pulling them further away from the steps leading to the hall. The torches were absent here, making it necessary to feel their way along the moss covered, damp wall.

"What are we looking for?" Harper asked, her voice barely above a whisper.

"There is a break in the wall down here that leads to the garden. It was to be used for escape in case of an attack. Few know of it. It hasn't been used for many years, but I grew up here. It should be about..."

Noise in the corridor behind them had them plastering themselves against the stones. Pounding boots and shouting echoed down to the women. Men cursed. They had obviously found Alex's body.

Shaking with terror, Harper pressed her lips together and breathed slowly through her nose. Knowing if they were caught, they would be immediately tortured and killed, Harper closed her eyes and tried desperately to remain calm. Reaching for Fenella's hand, she squeezed it to offer comfort. Neither woman moved, though Harper desperately wanted to scream.

"There?" Harper heard one man ask, guessing he was pointing in the direction the women had gone.

"Nay. 'Tis a dead end."

"Did ye see them leave?" the man demanded of another.

"I left the top of the stairs for only a moment to see if I was needed. They must have slipped through then."

The sound of a fist hitting bone followed by a thud reverberated as the offender was obviously struck as punishment for the offense of not seeing their captive leave.

Footsteps moved away and back up the steps. Air flowed back into Harper's lungs.

Fenella was slumped alongside her, exhaling her relief as well. Quiet descended once more.

Then Fenella whispered for Harper to help her push against the wall. The two pressed their bodies against the cold stone until it finally gave way just an inch. Continuing to push, the wall shifted another few inches and then little by little it grew wider. Points of sunlight dotted the filthy stones at their feet and Harper thought she had never seen anything so beautiful.

Peering out, Fenella looked to see if any guards were nearby, but all that was visible was a garden unattended by guards, underbrush, bare trees, and bushes. Stealthily, they eased their way past the opening into the foilage replacing the wall as it had been just in case someone remembered this exit.

Quietly, they edged along the trees, holding hands, alert for any noise.

Please let Daimh be here, Harper prayed silently.

***

The MacKenzies and the Forbes lined up just behind the tree line, shadows concealing their presence. Their swords were drawn and arrows nocked. Ian started forward when Daimh spurred his horse in front. "We cannot risk ye when we know of their treachery," he said to Ian.

"They would take great pleasure in killing the laird of Clan MacKenzie and ye would be a perfect target. I will make the demand."

Without waiting for Ian's certain objection, Daimh rode forward to the door of the castle.

"Clan MacKenzie has come to discuss terms," he shouted.

The door flew wide and a man with a furious expression stomped out. "Terms? Terms, ye say? Yer *galla* has killed Lord Alex and we know she has run to ye. Ye wish to discuss terms? I shall give you terms. Give over the woman and we will not kill ye all." The man retreated and the slamming of the heavy door echoed. Men appeared at windows pointing bows and arrows. They were not going to release Harper or give up without a fight. But Daimh savored the idea of killing any and all who had harmed his Harper.

Harper killed their lord? The baineann is even more remarkable than I imagined. But, then where was she?

A movement to his left in the distant foliage caught his attention. A bit of fabric waving in the wind, the red

195

color stark against the dark bark of a tree. It could only be Harper. The sheer relief he felt was like a drowning man breaking through the surface of the loch, gulping in fresh air. She was alive and, as far as he could tell, safe. Squinting into the splintered sunlight, he could see another was beside her, a slight girl, and no threat.

Without acknowledging what he had just seen, he spun his horse back to the line of men and approached Ian. "The lady Harper is hidden in the wood to the right."

Ian turned to John Forbes. "We have what we came for. Ye were kind enough to offer support, so I ask what ye need now so we may return the favor."

A slow smile lit John's face. "Take what is rightfully yours and go. We have enough men to see these cowards and miscreants regret their actions."

"And ye will enjoy it?" Ian asked, returning John's smile.

John shrugged. "Ye can't begrudge a man his pleasures."

The Forbes men moved forward as if stalking their prey. They knew they had no need to hurry, but soon the sounds of battle cries and metal clanging filled the air. Daimh was certain he heard John laughing in the distance and he shook his head. The man loved his battles, especially when he was the definite victor.

Daimh summoned Rory, and together they rode to where he had spotted Harper just outside the manor. Skimming close to the trees, Daimh extended his arm into the greenery and Harper grabbed for it. Taking hold, he hoisted her up onto the saddle and wrapped her in his arms, his joy knowing no bounds.

Behind him, Rory mimicked the same action and Fenella was lifted onto his horse.

Daimh spurred his horse forward, but as Rory made to follow, an arrow flew through the air and caught Fenella in the shoulder. She yelped and slumped forward and Rory scrambled to keep her mounted as he raced over to the others. Arrows flew around them, plunging into the ground and trees. But they were faster.

Then, as a group, the MacKenzies bid farewell to the Forbes and kicked their horses toward home.

***

Looking back and seeing Fenella had an arrow protruding from her shoulder, Harper let out a gasp.

"Daimh, we must save her! She protected me and I cannot let her die."

"Aye, my love. Let us ride away from the battle and we can see to her. The arrow landed high; she should recover. I am almost certain of it."

"Are ye hurt?" Daimh asked. "Did they harm ye?"

"Nay. But I am a mess."

Daimh laughed, the vibration in his chest comforting her. "Ye are the most bonny, the most *blasta*, the... I cannae find words to describe ye. But I must include brave. Ye survived and I am hoping ye hae not been harmed."

She knew what he meant. "No. I wasn't thanks to Fenella. You should have seen her. Alex was trying to... and she killed him. Hit him with a chunk of wood." Harper looked over at the girl cradled in Rory's arms in front of him on his horse. "She was so brave."

"Then I shall be forever in her debt."

"Are you sure she will be all right? I would never forgive myself if she didn't recover."

"Aye, we will see to it. I give ye me word." Wrapping her more tightly in his plaid, he nuzzled her neck. Shivers ignited her flesh, and she savored the feeling. If she'd had more energy, she would have exploded with pleasure. But exhaustion took hold of her as she nestled against him.

"Later, I need to hear what happened."

"Yes. I will tell you how stupid I was. But for now—I love you," she whispered.

He pressed her tighter against him. "I love ye, lass." He heaved a sigh. "But I fear we missed Hogmanay and our wedding date.

"Then we can celebrate when we return, right? Then if you still want to make me your wife, we can see it done as soon as we are home." *Home.*

"Aye. First thing."

"Well," she said, crinkling her nose, "after I have had a bath."

Chapter Nineteen

They rode hard, all anxious to gain some distance from Gordon lands. Although the Queen had promised the transfer to the Forbes, it had not yet been accomplished and there was still danger of attack until they crossed the border.

After several hours, they slowed the horses and edged into a wooded area. The slackening of the movement roused Harper and, feeling Daimh holding her, the immediate panic from her ordeal was replaced by warmth.

Daimh jumped from his horse, aided Harper down, and then approached Rory, reaching up to ease Fenella down into his arms. He carried her into a hastily erected tent and laid her on her stomach on a makeshift cot, Rory hot on his heels, clucking words of comfort to the girl. Harper was tight behind them.

Wanly smiling at Rory, Fenella was very pale and clearly in pain.

Rory turned to Harper, his expression begging. "Help her."

"I'll need some clean linen and water to wash the wound, she said to Rory." And raising her voice, "Does anyone have some whiskey?"

Harper pulled Fenella's filthy dress away from the

wound, and was relieved to see it wasn't very deep. Rory pressed a flagon of whiskey into her hand and, since the arrow was lodged in her shoulder in the back, she had to lift Fenella's upper body at an angle so she could drink. Taking a small sip, Fenella coughed, then groaned, but Harper coaxed her to take a few more draughts. Then, she helped the girl settle back while she soaked a cloth with the liquor.

"This will hurt, but briefly," Harper warned her.

Rory took the girl's hand. "I am here, lass. Just squeeze me hand when ye feel pain."

Harper suppressed a grin at the sweetness of Rory's gesture. *Already besotted*, she thought.

The color drained from the visible side of Fenella's face as Harper poured a bit of whiskey around the shaft of the arrow, but the girl did not cry out.

Harper took hold of the arrow at the base and carefully wiggled the head free. A glance at the clasped hands of Fenella and Rory, their knuckles white, confirmed the pain, but again, the girl did not even whimper.

Tears burned behind Harper's eyes, understanding that Fenella had suffered so much pain in her short life, this was probably nothing compared to what had left her swollen and bruised. She was glad Alex could no longer hurt his young wife.

There wasn't much bleeding; a bandage should suffice. When they returned to the castle, Freya could stitch it if necessary. Harper was no seamstress and hesitated to give the girl more discomfort.

Another few sips of whiskey and Fenella settled back, Rory at her side, and slept. Relieved that the danger was past, Harper slipped from the tent in search of Daimh.

Finding him in front of the fire in deep conversation with Ian, she hesitated to interrupt, but the need to feel him and have him reassure her was overwhelming. As she approached, Ian smiled at her and stepped away to give them privacy.

Daimh led her over to a fallen tree trunk and they sat, facing each other and holding hands.

"Tell me all," he coaxed.

Shaking her head, she sniffed. "All my fault. All my stupidity."

"Ye said as much before. What happened?"

He deserved to know. "Iona came to my bedchamber about midnight. I thought it was you, so I let her in. Then she said she had come to protect me. That you were her husband and Thomas your son."

Daimh's mouth dropped open in disbelief and hurt. "And ye believed her?"

"Not really. But I knew she was up to something, and she said she had proof and that I should follow her to the cottage. When she said that, I feared for Thomas's safety. I knew she wanted you and I also know the lengths some will go to get what they want."

Daimh digested this and nodded.

"I thank ye for worrying about the lad. That speaks of yer love for him." He pulled her hand to his mouth and kissed it softly.

"Then what?" he encouraged her.

"Once outside the castle, I was hit from behind. And woke up in the cell. After Fenella hit Alex, her husband— her very abusive husband—she led us out of the dungeon into the woods. And you know the rest."

"Aye. And what of Iona?" His eyes narrowed, his feeling about the other woman clear.

"Gone, according to Fenella. She ran off, afraid they would kill her."

"If they don't, I might," he said under his breath. "I am just so grateful ye are safe. And I hae no doubt the Forbes will make the Gordons regret their actions."

Ian stepped up to them and grinned. "I think I need to remind ye that the lass probably hasn't had a decent meal for a while, and I'll bet she could use a good rest. Me wife will hae me head if I bring her back in less than good shape."

Daimh jumped up as if he'd been burned. "Forgive me, my lady. Of course. Let's get you some food. And ye can sleep on me horse all the way back. I promise ye will not fall off."

***

As Harper entered the hall, Skye let out a very unladylike *whoop* and ran to her, squeezing her so hard Harper thought her sore ribs might crack. At her wince, Skye jumped back, horrified.

"Did I hurt ye. Forgive me. We were sick with worry. I'm just so glad ye're here. What did those *boidheaches* do to ye? Was it Iona? Did she betray ye to them and cause this? Come, ye must tell me all. But first, let's get ye a bath and some clean clothes. Ye smell like ye've been in a dungeon—I should know." This last was whispered. Then, as if just noticing Fenella leaning against Rory, she raised her eyebrows. "Who is that?"

"She saved my life. I will tell you everything, but a bath sounds wonderful. And are there any meat pies?"

Skye grabbed Harper's hand and led her to the stairs, asking that a bath be brought for Harper and for one to be put in the guest chamber for Fenella. "And some clean clothes for the lass."

Harper gratefully sank into the warm water and her muscles let go of some of the tension she'd been holding for days, Harper recounted the tale. As she spoke, Skye paced the room, going from one end to the other.

"I should have come to you or Ian, but it was late, and I was so stupid. I guess I was so afraid of something going wrong…"

"You weren't stupid. You were just going on past experiences. I probably would have done the same thing. And insofar as Iona is concerned, I knew it. I knew that witch was capable of evil. I could sense it. But I had no idea she would go so far." She stepped over to Harper. "I am just so grateful you are here."

Harper grinned. "Me, too."

"Now promise you will just ask someone next time. No, wait, we have to make sure there never is a next time." Skye nodded her affirmation to herself. "Well," she continued, trepidation pulling at her brow. "If you've had enough sixteenth century adventure, I'm hoping it hasn't changed your mind about staying."

"On the contrary. When I saw Daimh on the edge of that wood and he reached down to pull me up on his horse… I have never been so happy to see anyone in my life. And between that and my dearest friend being here, I cannot imagine going back to my dull life." She giggled. "Although I would be very happy to have no more such adventures. And maybe some Chapstick."

Skye ignored the joke and resumed pacing. "We must find Iona. She must be dealt with."

"Where I was taken is a long way away from here. Fenella said she overheard that Iona ran, but I don't have any idea where she could go. I am certain she wouldn't be welcomed here, and the Gordons have no more use for her."

"Aye, but I have no doubt she will find a way to survive and even find her way back here at some point. She might believe her mother will take her in."

"Would she? After what Iona has done?" Harper asked.

"A mother's love is not conditional. If nothing else, Eilidh might try and find a way to conceal Iona or help her find somewhere to go." Skye quieted in thought. "I shall ask Ian to speak to her. Putting you at risk as she did is certainly grounds for banishment or worse and Eilidh needs to understand that. And if she offers aid to her daughter, she will be guilty as well."

"I hope Iona doesn't put her mother in that position. Eilidh is a kind woman who does not deserve it."

"I agree. But Iona is not to be trusted. You of all people know that." Skye threw her arms in the air, palms out. "On a happier note, I believe we were planning a wedding before you were taken."

Harper grinned, joy filling her heart. "Yes. We were. Does it matter we missed Hogmanay?" She was sad that her capture had doused the festivities.

"Of course not. The celebration was merely postponed. And I will speak to—"

Neasa tapped on the chamber door and entered, a smile lighting her features and making her look years younger and prettier. She swept a bow to Harper, still languishing in the tub.

Harper broke out in a laugh. "I think the need for formality can be swept aside since I am not exactly in appropriate attire to receive company."

Now they all three laughed.

"We were talking about the wedding," Skye said.

"So many since ye arrived," she said to Skye. "Ye clearly brought so much love with ye."

"What a kind thing to say," Skye responded.

"But true," Harper agreed. "Skye is one of those people who makes life better."

Skye's cheeks reddened with her blush of pleasure. "You are both too kind. Now, the wedding."

"Aye," Neasa said. "We can make the preparations quickly, since we had already begun before…" She was clearly reluctant to mention what had transpired. There was no need to mention the ordeal further. "But it got me to thinking and I'd like talk to ye both aboot something." Her tone was so serious, Harper knew Skye was as concerned as she was.

Seeing their faces, Neasa smiled. "Oh, nay. Naught bad. Just an idea I've been toying with."

"And…" Skye encouraged.

"I've been thinking about Davina. Especially after Harper disappeared. And I hae a thought."

Both women looked at Neasa in question.

"I would like to… see her."

"See her?" Harper asked, confused. "But she is in the twenty-first century."

"I ken. I hae thought about some of the things ye both told me, and I would like to see that as well. For meself. And I could make certain Davina causes no more mischief."

"And how would ye do that?" Skye asked.

"I would say I was kin, which I am, and she has lost her mind. That would reassure no one would believe aught she says."

205

"She's in a coma and will probably stay that way," Harper said.

"I ken. But to see some of what ye described about things in the future. I would nae stay long. Just a few days. Ye both could teach me what I need to know and then I would come right back."

Neither Harper nor Skye spoke for a few minutes. Harper was imagining all the differences in life between then and now. It would be almost overwhelming.

"I do nae even ken if the cloak would work," Skye said. "And if it did, there's no guarantee ye could return. And if something were to happen and—well, I'd never forgive meself."

"Would ye be willing to let me try?" Neasa asked, the hope in her tone obvious.

"Would you wait until after the wedding? It shouldn't be too long until Daimh and I can wed and then…"

"And then you would be convinced you would never go back, so you'd have no need of the cloak," Skye said to Harper.

"Yes," Harper affirmed. The wedding to Daimh would make certain she never went back. She would be here, at Eilean Donan with Daimh and Skye… forever. Yes!

"Cloak?" asked Neasa.

Chapter Twenty

It was a dream within a dream. Harper hardly heard the words of the priest as she gazed upon her grinning groom. He leaned toward her, his smile highlighting his dimples, and she could barely catch her breath. He was so handsome. Dying in a dungeon had not been her fate. This was. Gazing into the eyes of a man she could love the rest of her life, a man who would love her in return.

The priest cleared his throat. "Do ye?" he prompted her.

"Oh yes," she responded happily.

And they were wed.

Daimh left her side only to bring her food and drink. The others danced and ate and sipped wine, the hall bursting with joy. After a few hours of revelry, Daimh took hold of her hand and, amid cheers and shouts, led her up the steps to what was now their chamber.

Closing the door, he stood with his back against it, just looking at her. Harper could feel the blush bringing color to her cheeks. A sigh and he took the few steps over to her, swept her in his arms, and gently laid her on the bed.

With his hands and his mouth, he worshiped her body and she returned the pleasures with her own hands and mouth. And when their bodies merged as one, she felt complete for the first time in her life. How could she have ever doubted the magic Skye had spoken of?

***

Dozing in contentment, Harper snuggled closer to her husband—*her husband*—reveling in the feel of his strong, beautiful body. It was pure bliss.

Suddenly, someone was knocking on their chamber door.

Daimh was up in a flash, cursing, annoyed if not downright angry at the intrusion, and wrapped his tartan around him. He cracked open the door as Harper pulled the linen cover up to her neck.

Eilidh stood trembling, weeping, at the entry. "Forgive me. Forgive me. She has him."

Daimh put an arm over the woman's shoulders, trying to calm her and have her make sense. "Speak plainly."

Inhaling on a sob, she shook her head. "Thomas. Iona is at the loch, and she has taken the lad, threatening to kill him unless ye denounce Lady Harper and agree to marry her."

Hearing this, Harper jumped from the bed and grabbed her clothes. She was beside Daimh in a heartbeat and together they followed Eilidh down the steps and out into the courtyard. They were quiet, unwilling to rouse others and expose the lad to public scrutiny.

Darkness laden with heavy mist cloaked their movements as they approached the gate. Challenged by a guard, Daimh raised his hand and just asked the gates to be opened. Unwilling to disobey, the guards did as told, and the three walked quickly away from the castle, Eilidh leading the way.

Iona sat on the opposite bank of the loch, speaking with Thomas who was rubbing at his sleepy eyes. At their approach, Iona stood and grabbed the lad, pressing him against her.

Loading the two women into a craft, Daimh rowed across in mere minutes and jumped out, moving cautiously to Iona and Thomas, the other two at his heels. Thomas jumped up to greet them, but Iona pulled him back down, her hand holding him firmly in place.

Iona pointed at Harper. "She needs to go."

"Give me me brother." Daimh spoke softly, but there was steel in his tone. Thomas struggled to get free, but Iona tightened her grip. "Stop squirming," she demanded.

"Make her leave," Iona repeated.

"Iona, give me me brother. Now."

"Nay. I will drown him first so I can hurt ye the way ye hurt me."

"I did nae mean to hurt ye, but ye cannae take it out on the lad. Step away from him and we can talk about this."

"Will ye marry me?" Iona demanded.

"If that is what ye need, I will send Harper away."

Although Harper knew he was saying the words only to gain the release of Thomas, it was unpleasant to hear. But she knew she needed to help.

"I will go. Give Thomas to his brother and I will go away, and you and Daimh can be together," Harper said, trying to sound convincing.

"Ye lie," Iona spat. "Nay. Ye will both suffer for what ye've done."

"Iona," Eilidh interjected. "Release the boy."

"As if I would listen to ye. Ye hae always loved him more than me. Nay. Ye will all suffer as I hae."

With that, Iona moved closer to the water, dragging

the boy with her. Then, angling her body for leverage, she lifted Thomas and tossed him into the loch. The water was not deep, but Harper feared the child couldn't swim.

Letting out a cry of anguish, Harper raced forward, cutting in front of Daimh, and jumped into the loch next to where Thomas flailed in the icy water. Eilidh screamed as Daimh splashed into the water behind Harper. Reaching Thomas instantly, Harper lifted his chin and he actually grinned at her.

"So verra cold," he said, his teeth chattering.

"It is. Come, let's go and get warm." Harper wrapped her arm across his chest and swam toward the bank, lifting him out into Daimh's arms. Daimh immediately cradled him and wrapped him in his plaid, then reached over to help Harper out of the loch. Pulling her against him, he hurried them both into the woods to Eilidh's cottage.

Daimh quickly stoked the fire as Thomas and Harper huddled together, warding off the chill. Without a word, Daimh was out the door, his running footsteps only obvious by the sound of breaking twigs.

***

Daimh found Iona and her mother on the crest of a grassy knoll just above the loch. Squinting in the early morning light, he could see the women talking. Eilidh's pleas for Iona to come back and face her punishment reached Daimh's ears. Iona violently shook her head.

He stalked forward, intent on capturing Iona, though he could not promise what he would do when he actually laid his hands on her. She had bargained away Harper to the Gordons for her own selfish gain and jealousy and

210

nearly cost Harper her life. The thought of his love being raped, tortured, and murdered was enough to drive him mad with rage. And then the witch had tried to drown Thomas. A child!

He watched as Iona slammed both her hands into her mother, forcing the older woman to fall to the ground. Then Iona took off running, looking over her shoulder to see she wasn't followed. Suddenly, she stumbled and fell forward, disappearing into the tall grass. Daimh came upon her, sprawled on her belly, her head at an awkward angle on a stone. Her lifeless eyes stared at nothing and a small amount of blood seeped from her temple. Eilidh rushed past him and fell to her knees next to her daughter, a cry erupting from her throat.

Tears rolled down Eilidh's cheeks and when she lifted her gaze to him, her expression was bleak with sorrow. "Forgive me. I had no idea she would go to such lengths. I would ne'er have let her near the lad if I'd thought…" She broke down crying and Daimh patted her on the back.

"I do nay blame ye. It is over. Come, I will take ye back to the cottage." And yes, it was over. Harper and Thomas were safe and Harper had shown herself to be strong and courageous. Why, she even jumped into the water to save Thomas when most wummen could nae even swim. His wife was one of a kind.

Eilidh shuffled behind him and when they reached her house, she rushed inside to cradle Thomas.

"He is warm now and fine. He was very brave," Harper said, trying to reassure the older woman.

"And so were ye," Daimh said, his tone reflecting his amazement. "Ye did not even think before risking yerself to save him."

211

"It was nothing," she responded. "I love Thomas and I cannot imagine him being harmed. Besides, we both needed a bath, right Thomas?"

The boy looked skeptical but managed a giggle.

Daimh turned to Eilidh. "I will send some men to retrieve your daughter and see her buried." Harper looked up at him in question. All he could do was shake his head. Iona was gone, no longer a threat to those he loved.

Eilidh nodded her thanks and held out the boy to Daimh, who took him in his arms. "Will ye be strong now while I take the lady back to the castle to get fresh clothes. And later, we can go riding. Would ye like that?"

"Ride horse?" Thomas shook his hands with excitement and had clearly forgotten his recent ordeal now that horseback riding was in the offering.

"Aye."

When Daimh and Harper were back in the small boat, he let out a sigh. "I wish there was a way to free him."

"Do you think there's any way the clan will ever accept him?"

"Nay. And I canna subject him to abuse. He hae suffered enough."

"Then we will have to love him enough for a clan."

"I love ye, wife."

"And I love you, husband."

Chapter Twenty-One

Harper had just changed into warm clothes when Skye knocked on her door, followed by Neasa.

"You wanted to see us?" Skye asked. "And how did ye get so wet?"

"Yet another adventure," Harper said. "Iona is dead. It was an accident."

Skye and Neasa sobered. "How?" Skye asked.

Harper related what had happened, and the other two women were aghast. "She threw the lad into the loch. To kill him?" Skye asked.

"What lad?" Neasa asked, completely confused. "Do I know naught of what goes on in me own house?"

Both Harper and Skye laughed. "No one knows. So you must keep yet another secret and we will tell you all," Harper responded. "But first, the reason I wanted to talk to you both... I've been thinking and maybe it's a good idea for Neasa to go and check on Davina."

Neasa's face lit up. "Truly?"

"Aye," affirmed Skye.

"We don't know if the cloak will still work and you may not be able to return, but if you still want to go..." said Harper.

Neasa clapped her hands. "Oh yes!" She hesitated. "Ye speak of a cloak."

Skye turned to Harper. "It does sound silly when spoken out loud."

Harper nodded and the two women laughed.

"What prompted this?" Skye asked.

"Iona. I guess I hadn't realized just how dangerous these women could be. I mean, going after me and Davina going after you, although terrible, was nothing compared to trying to kill a helpless child. I guess I just started to worry about what havoc Davina could cause if she woke up. And Neasa said she'd like to go…"

Skye took a deep breath. "I hate to think of denying Neasa her chance for adventure. But what would she do for money?"

"I actually brought some and put the rest of our stuff, including credit cards, in a storage unit. I could give Neasa my passwords to access my bank accounts if she needed more and she should be fine. It would only be for a short visit. Just time enough to get a taste of the future and check on Davina. A week or so?"

Skye pressed her lips together and faced Neasa. "There's much to learn. I wouldn't want you to freak out like Davina did."

"To what?" Neasa asked.

"Ah, you know… get very upset."

"Neasa, can you read?" Harper asked.

"Aye," she said.

"Then we can teach her and write down more. We can do this."

"Culture shock!" Skye said, still skeptical.

"I wish to try," Neasa said. "Not forever, o' course. Just for a sennight." Her enthusiasm was obvious.

"How long do you think we have before the cloak doesn't work or goes back to where it started?" Harper asked Skye.

She shrugged. "No idea. But I suggest we get to work."

And so begins Neasa's adventure...

About The Author

Leslie Hachtel has been working since she was fifteen and her various jobs have included licensed veterinary technician, caterer, horseback riding instructor for the disabled and advertising media buyer, which have all given her a wealth of experiences.

However, it has been writing that has consistently been her passion. She is an award-winning and Amazon bestselling author who has written eighteen romance novels, including thirteen historicals and five romantic suspense.

Leslie lives in Florida with her very supportive husband, and her writing buddy, Josie, the poodle mix.

She loves to hear from readers!

Website: https://www.lesliehachtel.com/

Facebook:
https://www.facebook.com/lesliehachtelwriter/

Twitter: @lesliehachtel

Blog: http://lesliehachtelwriter.wordpress.com

Bookbub:
https://www.bookbub.com/authors/leslie-hachtel